S0-AYA-641

Text copyright © 2021 by Nakisha "Shyne" Neal
All Rights Reserved.
Self-Published by Nakisha "Shyne" Neal

Printed in the U.S.A
ISBN: 978-0-578-24497-6

KARMA

"SHYNE"

This book is a work of fiction. Names, characters, places, and incidents are either a product of the author's imagination or are used fictitiously. Any resemblance to actual people. living or dead, events or locales is entirely coincidental.

KARMA

"SHYNE"

Dedication

This book is dedicated to my family. Everything I do. I do for you. Rest in Paradise. Johnella Young. We miss you Grandma.

KARMA

"SHYNE"

Introduction

It had to have been almost 3 a.m. I remember it being cold as hell. The night air whipped against my bare legs as I walked up the street to meet Mike. One of my local sponsors. Mike was married with a family, so picking me up at the house was not an option, plus I was only 16. I've been creeping with him for over a year now and whenever he called, he had $400 or better.

"Hey boo." He would say every time I saw him. It became part of the game acting as if he gave a fuck about me. "Boo, Really nigga." I wanted to say, but I played alone giving him a peck on his cheek. Even though Mike wasn't cute, and he was big as hell; he was my best sponsor at the moment. He paid for what he wanted with no problem. He wanted no disturbance in his home so if he wanted you, you would be well compensated. I like to call it hush money not that I would say a word that's not my style. "Where you wanna go?" he asked.

"God, I wish he would stop with the small talk, we both know where we're going, what we going to do, and how long we're gonna be there," I said to myself. "Holiday Inn," I said rubbing his legs as if I just couldn't wait to fuck him. "You want something to eat?" he asked. "Hell nah, is that all yo fat ass think about. I just want to ride yo little dick for the 5 minutes. You gonna last and get the fuck back to the house." that's what I wanted to say.

"No, I'm not hungry." I was getting disgusted but hey, a girl gotta do what a girl gotta do and Mike was quick, what I like to call easy money. I guess you may be thinking I'm a prostitute or a whore of some kind, but that's your opinion. I'm not laying down with nobody for free. I gots to get paid. I done gave away all the free pussy I'm gonna ever give up and the ones that got it. I hope they enjoyed it because it will never happen again. I wasn't always like this; I was made into this woman. You want to know how I got like this. I'll tell you.

At the tender age of 11, I was being molested by a family member. Which didn't make me grow up bitter and angry like most kids of sexual abuse. It gave me a high sex drive. By age 12, I was hot as a firecracker. That's how I got the nickname

"SHYNE"

Pepa. I wasn't having sex yet, but it didn't stop me from letting boys play in my twat and suck on my breast.

I had my first real boyfriend at 13. We were in love, at least I was anyway. His name was Jeremiah, and he was fine as wine. Everybody wanted him but he chose me and why wouldn't he? I was 5ft 2in. Caramel skin, and some people call me a redbone but I'm not that light. B cup breast, small waist, and an ass that sat up like a stallion. Not bragging or nothing but I had it going on! My high cheekbones and slanted eyes could lock down the attention of any man. I guess it wasn't enough for Jeremiah. He also preferred my friend Melanie or who I thought was my friend anyway. The bitch wasn't anything but a backstabbing snake. That's what I get for putting my trust in a man or rather a little boy. I caught this bitch fucking him at my house. No lie, I can't make this shit up. He broke my heart, yeah, I was hurt, but I got over it and vowed it would never happen again. I trust no one, no nigga, no bitch.

Now my girl Tameka is a different story. That's my round. You got a problem with her, you got a problem with me, and trust that's not a problem you want to have.

Tameka was short for her age. She was one of those small chicks, who, people would confuse for a child. She was gorgeous smooth brown skin and shapely to be small. She had long hair which made bitches hate because they were wearing weaves. We did everything together since 4th grade. We even got our cherries pop together in the same room. Neither one of us really had a lot growing up, but whatever we had we shared.

Bitches always had something to say about us, but haters make you famous. While they were hating, they should have been keeping their eyes on their man. If he was broke, you didn't have to worry about me no way, but if he had a little money then you may wanna put his ass on a leash. I never discriminate when it comes to a dollar sign.

A year after I broke up with Jeremiah's trifling ass for cheating on me. His brother Dirty started trying to holla at me. Now I told you Jeremiah was fine, but Dirty was (oh my God FINE). I know I should've felt bad, but given the circumstances I wanted revenge, and if he didn't care that I fucked his brother then why should I?

I was nervous because he was 8 years older than me, but I went alone anyway. He took me to a hotel out of town. I guess he didn't want to be seen with a minor. We got drunk and smoked weed all night. Of course, I gave him what we were there for. Before he dropped me off at home, he did something that blew me away, he gave me 200 dollars! I don't know what he was thinking. I ain't no prostitute, but he saw the look of confusion on my face. "Take it shorty, buy yourself something nice," he said.

"Wow," I thought to myself, 14 with 200 dollars I had struck it rich. I wanted to sleep with him again just to see would the same thing happen and guess what, it did. Dirty was my first sponsor. He was older so he taught me the game for what it was. He taught me my worth. Once I learned niggas would pay, I'd never be broke again. You better take it from me. One thing I know if he pays for it. He ain't gonna tell shit, cause if he does, I'll put his ass on blast. That's

"SHYNE"

why I only fuck with grown men, grown men don't tell.

That was back then, and this is now. I'm a grown woman now, 19 with no kids, I got my own house, black inside and out Lexus, the wardrobe of the year, and I didn't pay for any of it.

"Pepa." My girl Tameka calls my name. "I'm back here getting dressed," I yelled. "Get yo big ass out the mirror you're supposed to be ready. I told you I was on my way an hour ago, because I knew your ass was gonna have us late." Tameka was always nagging about my tardiness.

"I'm almost finished," I told her putting on my final touches of gloss. "Look in the closet and grab my black lace heels for me," I told her as I threw on my cream and black one-piece short set, that zipped up in the back, it showed off my big ass and wonderful curves. "Bitch hurry up we need to be on 78 by 11." She threw my heels on the bed with an attitude.

We were headed to Memphis for a night on the town. Which is what we did on the regular. We partied like rock stars and at the end of the night!

"SHYNE"

We would always end up at a local strip club. The biggest sponsors stayed in the strip club, and I was on the prowl for a new victim.

We decided to go to Pure Passion, we normally went to Ebony's Lace, but it was a Monday and that meant Monday Night Boxing. Niggas love to see naked women in a boxing ring. The place was packed. This was definitely the right choice for tonight. We made our way to VIP. The first time we ever came they harassed Tameka about her ID. One of the guys at the door slip security a few bills, mainly because he wanted to holla at me, and we haven't had a problem since. Now we just walked straight in like we own the joint. Some guy was always ordering us drinks or bottles. Some of the strippers hate but others understand the hustle. Hell, y'all hoes naked. How I'm gonna compete with that? But it wasn't gonna stop me from trying. The niggas with the most money sat ringside, and so did I. We watched a few fights and then I got bored.

"You ready to go?" I asked my girl. She looked at me sideways "Already? This gots to be a

"SHYNE"

record." She knew I would stay all night if I saw something I liked. She had a few hitters, so she didn't mind leaving early.

Then HE walked in, now this nigga took tall, dark, and handsome to a new level. When I say he was swaged out from head to toe. Versace silk shirt and white Versace slacks, Cartier frames, his wrist was icy and he only had one ring on his pinky finger. He would put you in the mind of puff daddy. Not looks but his swag, oh hell yeah. He must have been important; his presence commanded the attention of the whole room. Everyone gave him dap as he walked through the club to his ringside seats. He had a guy to his right who was also dressed in designer he must've been his main man, a couple more guys followed behind. 2 thirsty strippers flocked to him like he was a magnet. "Hold up Meek." I told her. She knew instantly what had caught my eye. "Sweet." She teases me.

Now everything in my mind was telling me to leave, call it a night. Something kept saying run Pepa, run like hell. This nigga is not for you, but it was something about him, something drew me to

"SHYNE"

him. My body wouldn't listen and why would it? He was the reason I came, so I ignored that little voice in my head, as us women normally do, and I made my move. "Work your magic bitch." Tameka said. And I did. I stood up grinding in slow motion to Usher's and Beyoncé's "Love in This Club" making sure he got a good look at my best assets. Pretending there was no one in the room but me and him. I've done this 100 times, so I knew he was watching. Hell, every nigga in the room was watching.

One of his associates comes over with a bottle of champagne. "My man would like for you and your guests to join him at his table. He also would like for you to have this." he handed me a bottle of

Dom Perignon. "Checkmate." "Tell him I'll buy my own bottle, but I will join him." I said with a smile. I didn't want the nigga to think I was thirsty or nothing, even if a nigga is a trick. All men love independent women. So, you trick them now, so they can trick on you

later. I winked at Tameka as we walked over to VIP God this man was even sexier up close. His neatly trimmed beard complemented his chocolate skin. A nigga this fine had to be bad news and I had no idea how bad.

I slid in right next to him. One of the strippers frowned, but she'll be ok. Now for the examination. See you have to pay attention to how a man carries himself, what type of clothes he wear, how his shoes look, and my favorite, how he smells? If he looks good and wears cheap cologne, then so is he. You ever heard the expression "I can smell a nigga with money." You better believe it. "Clive Christian, 1000 dollars a bottle. Works for me." As I took in his scent, "You want a lap dance?" tall dark and handsome asked.

As he motioned one of the strippers over to service me. Which let me know he had made up my mind for me. It wasn't my first lap dance. I wasn't a dyke or nothing, but I knew how to get my money. What you won't do, the next bitch will, so whatever he likes, I like and if he sensed I was scared of a little dance from a female, he might have written me off. That wasn't happening. I was gonna get what I came for. His home boy was

standing on top of the sofa or barely standing because he was so drunk popping bottles, throwing money and making a huge scene he was rich, and he wanted everyone to know! "Yo, son chill with all that dumb shit. We got company at the table" he told him. "Aight mane, you right. Ah Yo, we need more women over here," he yells out to the manger, before he turned up his bottle and took his seat.

"What up ma, what's your name?" Tall, dark, and handsome asked, paying close attention to how I reacted to the lap dance. "Ma" where the hell he from. I thought to myself. "Patrice but everyone calls me Pepa." I said "Pepa huh." He said licking his sexy lips. I normally don't get all hypnotized, but I couldn't control myself. His accent was thick every time he would say anything. I almost went crazy. I didn't know what he had but I wanted it.

"Get a hold of yourself Pepa. He's no different from any other nigga. Get his ass, then cancel

him, you got this." I nodded and watched him pull on his Newport. He definently was not from the South. "My name Vega." He said proudly like I should've known who the fuck he was. All I know is that his ass was loaded and all I cared about was how deep his pockets were. Little did I know it would be my worst mistake.
$$$$$$$$$$$$$$$$$$$$$$$$$$$$$$$$$$

    I was meeting my Aunt Denise for lunch at her favorite restaurant. I often took her out to eat because she was my favorite aunt. She worked hard but never had enough money at the end of the week. When her husband died it left her with huge responsibilities that she sometimes couldn't handle. So, I stepped in to spoil her. If I come across a nigga with some big bank, I would take her shopping mainly for a designer purse she loved them.

    "What's wrong with you?" My aunt asked. She caught me in my feelings it had been two weeks since I met Vega. It's never taken a nigga this long to get back to me. Who the hell did he think he was? Fake ass celebrity. I was tripping hard. Oh well fuck him, I'll just have to move on. Can't miss what you never had. Of course, I could've called him. He did give me his number too, but again who in the hell do he think I am. I will never call a nigga first. I don't give a damn how rich he is. If he's interested, he will call me. "Ain't shit T, just tired." I lied she thought I'd been in college for the last couple months. I loved my aunt to death. She was down to earth. I could tell her anything, but not this. I wouldn't be able to stand the look on her face if she ever found out. I never want her to be disappointed in me. I'll never hurt her like that. I was a strong independent woman who was on top of my shit and that's all she needed to know. I dropped out of school last semester. College had nothing to offer me. Going to school 4 years, and still might not get a job in my profession, waste of my time. I need that fast money in 4 years. I'll be rich and retired. "It will pay off, you'll see. Have you talked to your mother?" she asked knowing my answer "No not this week." I told her. "You should call her." She said. "I will just not now." I told her. Me and my mother were like vinegar and oil we did not mix. We got alone just to get along. My mom kicked me out as soon as I graduated high school. I've been on my own ever since. She was too controlling and only saw things her way. I don't play by anyone rules, but my own.

"I said call her Pepa." She meant business. Even if I didn't care for my mom. That was still my mom and her sister and she didn't play about her. She always thought she would be the one to mend our messed-up relationship, but we were too much alike.

I grab my phone out of my Saint Laurent bag to call my mom. When it starts to vibrate, Vega popped up on the ID. "saved by the bell." I said

"Hello" I answered in my sexiest voice. My aunt just shook her head and went back to eating. She know how I gets down.

"What you got going on sexy?" his voice made me squirm in my seat.

"Having lunch with my aunt." I swirl my straw,

"What's on your mind?" I asked him.

"SHYNE"

"You" he answered. "I can't tell." I smiled hard. "Come kick it with me." He demanded.

"When?" I bit on my bottom lip.

"Now" he said. I loved a man who thought he was in control, but I had to see where his head was. Make sure we were on the same page. Making sure I wasn't wasting time that I didn't have. So, I gave him a little test.

"I'd love to baby, but I was with my girl the other night. My car is out of commission." I lied.

"Tell ya girl if she bring you to me. I'll take care of her; you got my word. Or I'll come get you. Either way I'm gonna see you today." He said. I was really grinning now.

"We'll be there." I hung up. "I gotta go auntie." I gave her the money for our meal, kissed her cheeks an flew. "Handle that" she smiled "And call your mother," She shouted to my back. "I will. I promise." I had no intentions of calling my mother. Instead, I called my girl Tameka and told her get dressed it was time to ride, plus Vega had a tip for her. As usual she was down to ride.

"SHYNE"

"Girl you know I'm with the shit. I need to holla at dude I met last week anyway he been begging me to come see him." She said

Tameka had a man at home, he was pretty good to her too. His name was James. They had been together since high school and shared a twoyear-old daughter. Bitches always was telling him shit about Tameka doing this and that. He didn't listen ever since he almost lost her by asking for a blood test for their daughter which turned out to be 99.9% his child. He didn't indulge in anymore gossip about her, he loved her. Which is one reason he lets her walk all over him.

Now me on the other hand, he hated. Hell, it wasn't my fault that she was out acting as if she had no man, cheating and shit, yeah maybe it was, but she's a grown ass woman. The only bitch I trust by my side. Yes, I'm selfish and we already know that.

His sister's Enisha and Kela hated us both couldn't stand the air we breathed. They knew his ass was whipped and it wasn't a damn thing they could do about it. Tameka was constantly arguing

"SHYNE"

with them and twice we all met up and banged, but once they finally realized he wasn't leaving her alone. They backed off.

Vega gave us the directions and we were on our way. The ride to Memphis seemed so long as my girl talked my ears off about nonsense mainly on how Vega could be the one. "Yea right, so could the Pope." I'm really gonna take relationship advice from you. Tuh, girl take your own advice. I guess she just want me to be happy with one man, but that shit is not in my DNA. We pulled up to Vega's house. "Nice to see you again." Vega hugged me and invited me into his home. He had to have been born in Versace it fits him so well.

The 3-bedroom home was not what I expected. It was nice but not as nice as he was. 3 of his boys were in the front room playing Madden on the XBox, Antwan, Zae and Kahlil who they called Capone I could imagine what that meant. Antwan was really cute, light skin, and slim with gold teeth. Zae was dark skin and had a body out this world. He was always dressed in silk like Vega. Capone had it going on fine, caramel skin, hazel eyes, and his jet-black hair lay down in waves across the top of his head. He had a muscular build and he was covered in tattoos.

Me and Tameka walked in and took a seat at the bar. Vega fixed us both a drink.

"I hope you guys brought some party clothes, if not I'll have my man run you guys by the mall. Capone throwing a biker's boys party tonight. Young Jezzy is performing. It's gonna be lit." He told us.

Capone rode bikes. He lived and breathed it. He also sold dope, but he made major bread racing his bike.

Vega peeled off 1000 dollars and handed it to Tameka. She tucked it neatly in her bra. We heard an argument taking place in the front between Zae and Antwain.

"Hell, nawl nigga, put my fucking money back," Zae.

"Nigga how the fuck you sound, put yo money back, nigga you lost. I'm tired of whooping on you anyway. You done lost 10 bands today. Let it go." Antwain.

"Bet back" Zae pulled out a rubber band knot.

"SHYNE"

"NO" Antwain said laughing as he stood up to leave.

"You just gonna take that. Nigga you must be hard up. I'll give you more than that. Didn't know you was fucked up out here like that. Take my money and run. You can have it though." Zae said cocky

"Take it nigga. I gets money. I ain't taking shit. Yo V, you need to get yo boy. I won this money." Antwain pulled out his winnings to flash them.

"Yo chill with that shit. Capone get them niggas" Vega said.

"These niggas stupid. Don't know why Ant keep betting this nigga anyway. He hate to lose," Capone said.

"Fuck you nigga." Zae.

"Fuck you." Capone replied. Zae reached for his gun. He hated to be embarrassed. He was young, rich, hotheaded and trigger happy which was the main reason Vega kept him around. He was getting money no doubt, the whole crew was, but Vega bought most the clothes he wore on GP.

"SHYNE"

Zae looked up to Vega. One day he would be Vega.

"Nigga you bet not never pull a gun in my fucking house what's wrong with you." Vega said before Zae could pull the gun.

"I wasn't gonna shoot the nigga." Zae played it off.

"If you shoot me nigga you better shoot to kill" Capone said standing.

"V, I'm finna dip before I have to fuck baby Vega up over here." Capone said to piss off Zae.

Everyone knew he wanted to be just like Vega. Zae was biting down to keep quiet. "You out my nig, see Zae you always running my company off." Vega joked "Yea me too, I'm out." Antwan and Capone gave him dap before they left the house. "What I'm gone do with you." He threw his hand up at Zae. Me and Tameka just sitting back watching the show. After we chilled another 30 min.

Vega had Zae run us to the mall. Me and Tameka both coped matching Coogi dresses and heels for tonight. Zae walked behind us texting in his phone as we tore the mall down shopping. He took care of the bill in each store we went in. We had no limit, no budget. I was blown away. Never had I seen any shit like this. How much money were these niggas playing with? Zae had taken a liking to Tameka the way he was throwing around money he has my vote. While she was getting to know him, I was getting close to Vega. He was so damn sexy to bad I would have to drop him soon 90 days was my limit for a so-called relationship. I didn't want to get too attached, plus he already wasted 2 weeks bullshitting.

"What's wrong with your car ma?" he asked. I looked surprised. I had forgotten I told him my car wasn't running.

"I think it may need an alternator or something, you know if it ain't one thing it's another." I lied.

"You let someone check it out?" he asked. "Not yet." I said,

"What's the hold up?" he asked "I drive a Lexus. Can't no shade tree look at that. I'm waiting on my dad to send me some money from Atlanta." I lied.

"SHYNE"

My father does live in Atlanta, but I ain't asking his cheap ass for nothing. He always gives me the 3rd degree before he sends it. "Patrice you think money grows on trees. You need to be more independent, and stop being so lose with yo money. Blah blah." So, I stop asking a long time ago. "We'll see what we can do about that. You get high?" he asked blowing smoke from his nose.

"I only smoke loud." I said knowing he had some pressure. "Funny, do I look like a lame." He passed me the blunt smiling.

We small talked a little. I learned he has a 9year-old son, and just as I suspected, he's from New York. 26 years old even though he never said it, I knew he was a major boss and was into some very illegal shit. Nobody really knows the story about how he ended up in Memphis with no family only his boys. Rumors circulated that he killed his plug and was wanted for murder in New York, but then they say that about everyone from out of town.

His connect was out of Jackson, MS. He also had a plug in Miami, and he had another house there also. Zae ran the drugs out of Miami and Capone ran Memphis because he grew up on Trigg, a street in South Memphis known for heavy drug traffic.

At the club I got a few stares, but I was used to that. Vega bought bottles all night we had enough sparklers going off to start a fire. It was Capone's night. I just wished someone would've told Zae as usual he was belligerent, but no one seemed to care they let him do him. Everyone was having a good time.

This was some real-life celebrity shit we had the whole top floor overlooking the club. Zae started throwing 100 dollar bills off the balcony just to see the crowd go wild he must've thrown 20 thousand away. Capone and his crew were in black and orange leather jackets Sunset Riders on the back. They were also in VIP with us. Other biker groups were there to show their support also. As the night ended and we got ready to walk out the door I pretended not to see a dispute between Vega and another woman. Hell, he wasn't my man.

We made it back to Vega's house around 3:30 am. Tameka went to the backroom with Zae.

"SHYNE"

While I stayed in the living room with Vega. We do this all the time, nothing new. She knew not to bother me, and I knew the same GET THE MONEY.

"Make yourself at home Ma." Vega said we were both tipsy as hell. I sat on the sofa and pulled off my Coogi heels. He came back with a plate of cocaine and 100-dollar bill on it. Coke wasn't my thing but who was I to judge the next man. He hit a line like a pro, then passed me the 100-dollar bill. I shook my head to say no. He shrugged his shoulder, pressed his thumb against his nostril, and hit another line.

"You feeling me Ma, his eyes were glazed looking from the drugs.

"Of course." I lied. This was the part I always hated; men did nothing but lie. I'm not that bitch you have to lie too. Give me and I'll give you. A shared experience.

"Take your shirt off Ma let me see them things unleashed." Vega said. I didn't mind showing off my body, my breast sat up at attention even without a bra.

"Damn Ma." He said admiring my artwork. "Come here." He grab me by my waist placing me

"SHYNE"

on top of him now my B cup breast were directly in his eye view.

He poured cocaine on them just to lick it all off. In no time, we were rolling around in the living room like no one else was in the house. I was seated on the sofa, my legs wide open as Vega licked cocaine off my wet and throbbing clit. I didn't know what he was doing to me. I've had my pussy sucked before but never had I felt so good in my life or maybe I was high from the coke he kept inserting in me. Either way I was gonna enjoy this ride. All that mattered now was the feeling. The feeling as I was flying above the clouds. I started massaging his head to let him know he was doing a great job.

"Don't stop. Don't stop." Was all I could say as I released juices all over his sofa. Vega knowing, he had satisfied me. Raised up and dropped his pants to reveal his thick erect penis. I knew the boy was packing but damn, I wanted to make an exit no lie.

"What the fuck he gonna do with that. I know this shit ain't gonna last long. This nigga not bout to stretch out my insides." I thought to myself, but I was no pussy and definitely no stranger to dick. Without missing a beat, I took a deep breath like it was my last and took him into my mouth. Not bragging or nothing but my head game alone was a weapon. I could easily have a nigga eating out the palm of my hands. That's why it was only a selected few.

Whoever got it.

With all the money I saw Vega flashing, he was definitely going on the hit list. His head was thrown back and his eyes rolling in the back of his head as I sucked his dick like a maniac, trying my best to deep throat it without choking. I got mad skills and no gag reflex. Super head ain't got shit on Pep! "I want that pussy." Vega grabbed me with force laying me on my back. My ass was halfway off the sofa as he slid his thickness inside me. You could hear the sounds of wetness as he stroked in and out of me. It was painful but pleasurable. I had to admit the boy was fucking me so good. I was begging him to stop and keep going at the same time. As much coke as he snorted, he could probably last all night and yes, he did. Was it worth it. Hell yeah. Feels good to be fucked good every once in a while, most times I be ready to get it over with but not tonight, Vega you are it baby take your time. After we finished, we showered and watched T.V. until Tameka was ready. I wasn't gonna rush her. He wanted me to stay all night but when Tameka come out the room, she was ready to get home. I guess she didn't get the same fucking as I did, plus the sun would be up soon. Vega gave me 3,000 dollars to get my car fix. Tameka said nothing the whole ride home. I fell asleep in the passenger seat.

$$\$$$

The ringing of my doorbell woke me up. "I'm coming. I'm coming." I said half asleep and hungover. I looked out my peep hole and it was the devil herself. I unlocked the door for my mother. Her shoulder length bob flowing and bouncing as she walked in. Her petite frame wrapped in Prada from head to toe. She looked around at my apartment in disgust like it smelled of rotten cheese and piss. I just rolled my eyes behind her head. Bitch you been out the hood 5 minutes and now you claustrophobic.

I mean, my place was decked the fuck out. My living room furniture alone cost 18,000 dollars, but I guess it's not good enough for Mrs. Melissa Kirks. My mother was now married to the biggest, crookest attorney in the state of MS. My mom was the biggest gold digger of them all. She bagged his ass and now she wanted to be all high class. 2 years before they were married, she worked in his office as his "assistant." Christopher's wife died from cancer a year later. She wasn't lukewarm in the ground before they were engaged and momma had redecorated the poor woman's house.

"What's up momma?" I asked. I didn't have time for her shit today.

"Well, you would know if you bothered to answer your phone or call me back instead of having me drive across town to deliver you a message." She removed her Prada sunglasses rolling her eyes.

"Ma you could've just texted me." I slammed the door that she left wide open and walked over to the kitchen to make my morning coffee.

"Is that right Ms. Thang, I thought you would like to know your father's in the hospital." She said nonchalantly.

"Why? What happened?" I asked. concerned. "Lung cancer, he's going to die Patrice." She says having no concern for my feeling. She could be such a bitch at times. She would do shit to see me break, but I wouldn't give her the satisfaction.

"How do you know that ma?" I asked paying her no attention my father smoked like a chimney every day of his life, so I can't be too surprised that he would end up with cancer.

"I just talked to his wife." She frowned. She hated my dad's wife Terri. "They're just waiting on you to arrive before they pull the plug."

I almost dropped dead myself. This was really happening. My father was about to die, but if I knew anything, I knew that wasn't my mother's reason for being there. She could care less if my father rot in an open grave. She searched my face for emotions. I kept my poker face. I swear, sometimes visits with my mother felt like dying a slow, painful death.

"Do you need me to drive you?" She asked. "No, I'll be fine." I said.

"Their reading the will tomorrow." She said. Ok, now we getting somewhere. Now you think I'm money hungry. It's in my DNA. I get it from my momma.

"And. What?" I said aggravated and she knew it.

"Don't sass me little girl. I just want to make sure you get what's yours." She said. I wanted to burst into laughter. It was becoming harder and harder to keep a straight face. "You don't want those boys and their momma to steal all the money. You are the oldest, and you should get more. I know your daddy left you a nice amount of money." She said.

"Ma that's why he has a will. It will be fine; I'll call you when I get back home." I happily let her out and packed my suitcases for Atlanta.

My phone ranged it was my aunt. "You ok baby girl?" she asked. "Yeah, I still can't

"SHYNE"

believe it. Even though we had our ups and downs, lord knows I'm gonna miss him." I said.

"I know you will. Do you need anything?" she asked.

"Nawl, I'm about to get on the road. I'm about to see if Meek want to ride with me." I said.

"Ok baby, mwah." She blew me a kiss threw the phone. "Love you too." I hung up.

I'd been calling Tameka, but her phone kept going to voice mail. Something was going on with her and when I got back to town, I would make it my business to find out. The hospital room was crowded with friends and family. My father lay in his hospital bed not knowing in a few minutes he would no longer be a part of this world. His wife cried aloud by his side, and my grandmother Johnella held her hand.

I watched silently as he took his last breath. That was the first time I saw someone die, but it wouldn't be the last. I stayed in Atlanta for the funeral. My father was a well-respected person in the community, so there were a lot of people in attendance. I was seated on the front row along with my 2 brothers and Terri.

"SHYNE"

My father left me a nice amount of change, that I couldn't touch until I was 25. My mother is gonna love this. I couldn't wait to call and let her know. She called my father everything but a child of God. She wasn't concerned about my pain. Only the fact that there was no money at the time. I guess that's why my father always wanted me to be more responsible with my money. He knew when he died, I'd inherit a quarter million dollars.

$$$$$$$$$$$$$$$$$$$$$$$$$$$$$$$$$$$$
Vega called while I was on my way back to Mississippi.

"How are you beautiful." He knew how to make me smile.

"I'm good, leaving Atlanta." I said
"Ah, yeah what you doing there." He asked.

"My father's funeral." I answered.

"I'm sorry to hear that. Are you ok?" he asked,

"Honestly I don't know." For some reason I wanted to be with him. I felt safe with him my father was gone. For the first time in my life, I felt alone.

"You get your ride fix?" he asked.

"Yeah." I answered

"You feel like coming to see me. I got something for you." I knew I was going I loved surprises.

"I'll be there." I hung up.

I stopped by Tameka's crib to see what was up with her. Her boyfriend James came to the door. He couldn't stand me. He just put's up with me because of Tameka. James was a cute chocolate man. Tall and had a nice body. I never understood the reason she always cheated on him.

"Hey, James Meek here?" I asked. He didn't even speak back just yelled out her name.

"Hey Pepa." She came into the kitchen as if she hadn't been avoiding my calls.

"Where you been, I been calling you all week?" I didn't have time for the small talk.

"I lost my phone, just went and got a new one yesterday." I could tell she was lying, but for my own selfish reasons I dropped it.

"SHYNE"

"Sorry to hear about your Dad. I tried calling you this morning." She said.

"I just turned my phone back on a few hours ago. You sure you ok Meek?" I asked.

"Yes, I'm cool." She assured me "I'm your best friend. If there was anything wrong or anything I did, you would tell me right?" I said

"Of course, I would. I'm fine. I just lost my phone. That's it." She said "Ok then, I'm bout to go meet Vega. I think I'm gonna stay a few days in Memphis to clear my head. My dad left me money, but I can't touch it till I'm 25." I said.

"And your mother." She raised a brow. "You know she pissed." We both laughed, knowing how money hungry my mother could be.

"I'll see you later." I turned to go out the door. She called my name.

"Pepa." I turned around.

"Yeah." I said, "Be careful." She said sincerely. Something really had her spooked. "Always." I left her house. I went home packed 3 of my Louie suitcases and headed to Memphis. I checked into the Laquinta Hotel. I knew I wouldn't be there long. The kind of man Vega was, he wouldn't let me stay one night in a hotel, but you know me. I'm always playing a role.

"Where you at ma?" He called.

"I just got in town. I'm at the Laquinta unpacking my suitcases." I told him

"Come again. I know you just didn't say you was at a hotel." I expected this reaction.

"Yea I planned on staying for a few days and." He interrupted me "Don't insult me ma, text me which Laquinta. I'm on my way to get you." He hung up not giving me a chance to respond. I texted him the address, and 25 minutes later him and his boy Capone were at my door.

"Let's go." He ordered me like I was a 3-year-old child. "Give Capone your keys. You gonna ride with me." He said. I did as I was told. We left in Vega's midnight blue SLR McLaren Benz. We drove to Vega's house, only this wasn't the same house as last time.

"Who's house?" I asked.

"Mine." He said. His house was like something out of a magazine. Huge with a gated entrance. 6 car garage and swimming pool.

"SHYNE"

I also found out that Vega promotes concerts and bike shows, but I doubt that's how he makes his money. Inside his home he had pictures of him taken with every celebrity from Madonna to Biggie Smalls. I'd never met anyone like Vega before. I started to wonder would I be enough for him or was he out of my league.
"This is for you." He said. I spotted the red gift bag and my eyes lit up.

"What is it." I took the bag.

"I don't know." He walked away to the bar. I eagerly open the bag and pulled out the black box. "Cartier" I thought to myself, staring at the silver watch with pink diamonds.

"This had to have been 20 G's?" I looked at him surprised.

"47 to be exact. I got it at a discounted price, from my jeweler." He said like it was nothing.

"47 thousand dollars." I held it like I was scared to put it on.

"Yes, now put it on. I want to see ya blinging." He smiled "What the fuck! Now I know he's out of my league. This type of shit only

happens in Ashley and Jaquavis books." I
thought to myself as I put on the watch.

"Thanks." I said,

"No need for that." He smiled

"Where did he take my car?" I asked. "He'll
bring it by later. I know you're not planning on
leaving, are you?" He looked up from his glass of
Patron and pineapple.

"Nawl, just asking." I said.

"You want a drink?" he asked.

"Sure." I slid on the bar stool, looking
around admiring his house everything looked so
expensive. I couldn't keep my eyes off Vega
either.

"So, who's house were we at a couple
weeks ago?" I asked.

"Mine, you sure ask a lot of questions, you
the folks?" he raised a brow.

"Nope, are you?" I snapped

"I might be, never know these days." He
handed me my drink.

"So, you want to kick it this weekend, I got a
couple shows lined up if you want to party. I
know your pops just died. I'm here for you ma."

"SHYNE"

He said lifting my chin, it brought a smile to my face. I didn't want to party. All I wanted was for him to hold me. I just wanted to be in his arms.

"Can we stay here?" I asked.

"Sure ma, we can do that too." He hugged me.

"You hungry?" he asked.

"Not really" I answered but I really hadn't eaten much.

"You need to eat ma. I'm gonna call Capone and tell him to bring us some take out when he brings your car." He picks up his phone. I guess I didn't realize how hungry I was. I ate all of my food. If it wasn't a shame, I would've eaten his too. Vega fixed me a bubble bath, washed my whole body. Dried me off then lay my naked body on his silk sheets. I saw him admiring my me. My eyes screamed for him to touch me. He lay beside me all night holding me tight until I fell asleep his arms.

$$$$$$$$$$$$$$$$$$$$$$$$$$$$$$$$$$$

"SHYNE"

"The nigga crying, he need more time." I woke up to voices downstairs. I was trying to make out what they were saying. "What the fuck he mean? It's been a month already; who this nigga think I am the bank?" Vega said.

"Princess." He called out.

"Yes." She answered.

"Go back to see that nigga in 30 minutes if he ain't got my Guap. Send that bitch to see the Easter bunny." Vega commanded.

"You got it, Boss." Princess said

I walked on downstairs Vega, Capone, and a white female were seated in the front room. I assumed she must've been Princess. She was a slim looking white girl who looked mean and sexy at the same time, a real Angelina Joline looking chic. She had her long blonde hair pulled into a bun. She wore all white Dolce and Gabbana pants suit, red bottom heels, and Fendi frames over her eyes.

"Hey ma, you woke?" Vega noticed my presence. Everyone turned in my direction.

"SHYNE"

"Pepa Princess, Princess Pepa, and you already know Capone." He introduced us to each other I nodded with a slight smile she did the same. Then, Vega gave them the eye to let them know the meeting was over.

"You ok ma." He noticed my demeanor. I didn't know what the hell I was getting myself into.

"Yeah, just tired. I didn't realize how tired I was. I hadn't really slept in a week." I said

"Yeah, yo ass was out like a light. I got breakfast waiting on you." He grab me by the hand and walked me into the large kitchen where he had pancakes, bacon and eggs waiting on me. I didn't know what to say. Vega was the best! "God this man is so sweet. I know it's too good to be true. If I'm dreaming, don't ever wake me up." I silently prayed.

"So, what do you want to do today?" He took his seat.

"I got a bike show this evening. I'll swing you by the mall so you can cope something to wear." He said,

"SHYNE"

"I brought clothes." I told him. I didn't know what was happening to me, "I brought clothes." Where the fuck did that come from. I loved to shop.

"I got you ma. Don't worry about nothing your superman is here." He placed his hand across his chest. I smiled. The man sure could keep a real smile on my face, but I couldn't get my mind off the situation from earlier. What was this nigga really into? Damn why did I always have to be so thirsty. I knew I needed to take my ass home, but I was having way too much fun. Vega was way too much interesting.

The racetrack was none like I saw in the small towns in Mississippi. My life was like a movie for real. We were seated in the sky box. It had reclining seats, a bar, and complementary food. Vega grab a pair of binoculars and went over to talk to a well-dressed white man in the corner. Vega was right about one thing; I am nosey as hell. I pretended. Not to pay them much attention as a watched the bikes race through my binoculars. Never understood why pay thousands for a seat and you can't even see from up here.

KARMA

"SHYNE"

But oh well, it's not my money. Vega and the guy pretended not to know each other as they pretended to have light quick conversation, but if I knew anything, it was body language and energy. Yes, he definitely knew
this man, maybe he was the plug. Vega puffed on his Cuban cigar, as he walked back over to me.

"I need to go down by the tracks, your welcome to stay up here until I get back or you can come alone your choice." Vega.

"I think I'll come alone." I definitely was going wherever he went. Nigga, I don't know you well enough for you to leave me in a room full of white people.

We exit the skybox and went down to where the common folk were. Now this my type of party down here. Point me to the negro wing. We came up on the backside of the tracks, weed and cigarette smoke filled the air. People were selling BBQ plates and fish plates. Vega was the guest of honor. Everyone was trying to talk to him or just be near him and I was on his arms. I felt like a boss, a real lady boss. I was used to being with ballers and being spoiled by men, but Vega was not your average baller.

"You enjoying yourself?" He asked.

"Yes." I said.

"Let me know when you ready to leave." He kissed my jaw and walked away to talk to Capone and Zae who were close to the tracks. Capone was getting ready to race next. Capone biker's name was Torque because of his speed on the track. We watched his race. I watch Vega bet 100 thousand dollars on Capone and I watched him collect his winnings.

We made it to Vega's place around 1:30 in the morning, both of us feeling really tipsy. I flopped down on the sofa turning on the 82" flat screen T.V. Vega once again brought a plate filled with coke to the table with $100 bill. I watched him as he hit a line of coke and sniff really hard. Rubbing his nose. By the look of Vega, you would never expect he was a drug user. I heard of functioning addict like him, who could get high and still make money.

He passes me the bill; I shook my head to tell him no.

"SHYNE"

"You sure, this shit makes you feel Mad good ma." I didn't know why or what made me want to try the coke. Maybe I was morning my father. For some reason, I wanted to please him. I wanted him to feel as if I wasn't judging him. I wanted to be his one and only love. His ride or die bitch.

"I don't know how." I said nonchalantly. He fixed me up a small line.

"Put the bill close to your nose and lightly sniff its easy." He said placing my fingers around the bill. "What the hell are you doing." I said before I sniff the coke. My nose was now on fire as I was blowing, hoping to reverse the effect. Now regretting my decision. The lights in the room became brighter. It was as if my eyes were open for the first time. I could hear every noise in the room from the clock ticking to the drip, from the kitchen faucet. Only I couldn't make out what Vega was saying 2 feet from me.

"WHAT?" I yelled, letting him know I couldn't understand what he was saying. My eyes bucked. I could see him smiling as if it was funny.

KARMA

"SHYNE"

This reaction, he must've seen before he knew I was fucked up.

"You good ma?" he asked.

"My nose burning." I frowned rubbing my nose, my eyes, whatever to get a feeling. My whole face felt numb. He could see I was about to flip out.

"Relax." He grabs my hand.

"This shit burns," still rubbing my nose trying to feel my face. Now bitter snot was sliding down the back of my throat. I wanted to spit it out. I started frowning.

"You feel that?" he asked. I guess referring to the slime in my throat.

"What? it's supposed to do that. What is it?" I knew I sounded dumb like I shouldn't even be here.

"A drain, you will get used to it." He said, "Use to it, I don't like that part, but you were right I do feel good."

He fixed me another small line of coke. I hit it lay back on the sofa trying to enjoy the slime going down the back of my throat. I couldn't be

"SHYNE"

still for long. I felt like I could fly. I felt as I had the strength of 10 men. I stood up dancing to the music in my head, because there sure, as hell was none playing. "That's its ma, let loose." Vega cheered me on. The more he cheered, the bolder I became.

I started taking off my clothes. I don't know why it seems like the right decision at the time. Vega was all eyes he helped me to another line of coke. As I rub on my clit for him. I never felt so good in my life. I should've been tried this shit. I felt like super woman. I never wanted this feeling to leave me. I watched as Vega assaulted my pussy with his mouth. The night went black.

I woke the next morning or I think it was the next morning, I'm not sure. I was naked in Vega's bed, but I don't remember the past details. My head was spinning, my mouth felt as if I'd been eating sand and I most definitely needed to take a shower. "Vega," I called out "Vega," I called out again he didn't answer. He must've been gone. I drug my stiff body out of bed and into the bathroom to take my shower.

"SHYNE"

Vega's bathroom was dope, his tub was in the floor like Tony Montana's in Scarface real gold trimmed almost every inch of the bathroom. As I was getting ready to take a bath, I heard Vega come into the room. "I'm in the bathroom." I said through dry lips. I dropped my robe to get into the water, if I could just feel it, I knew my body would feel better.

I turned to see Zae standing in the doorway his hands rubbing his privates. Staring at me like a piece of steak. I was so embarrassed. I immediately grab my robe to cover myself. "What the fuck you doing in here?" I asked him. He said nothing and just gave me a wild look. I decided I would walk past him if I could just get to the door. He pushed me back into the bathroom.

"That pussy must be made of gold, if Vega got you here this time of morning." I looked at him sideways.

"What the hell, where is Vega?" I tried to stand my ground, but I was terrified. The look in his eyes let me know we were doing it his way and his way only. He was in full control.

"SHYNE"

"He's not here, but don't worry I got you." He gently caressed my cleavage then opened my robe to revel my naked body. "Um." He licked his lips looking like a rapist. I tried to snatch away from him that's when shit got real.

He grab my face forcing his tongue in my mouth. The taste made me want to throw up. I bit the hell out of him. He slaps me so hard I flew into the wall and bust my nose.

"I love a hoe that puts up a fight, all you money hungry hoes are alike." He said grabbing me by my throat dragging me to the bed. He was calling me every whore in the book as he was strangling me with one hand and unfastening his belt with the other. It was like he was getting turned on. "Please don't do this." I was trying to get the words out. The more I tried to talk, scream, or move the tighter his grip got. My nose bleed all over the sheets. I clawed at his strong arms for him to let me loose, but it didn't help.

"You think you the first bitch I did this to ask yo girl about me. She put up a fight, but in the end, she liked it and so will you." He spit in his hand to rub it on his erected penis to force himself inside me. I cried as I struggle to push him off me. Just when I lost strength to fight him anymore, I saw Vega and Princess entered the room. Vega struck Zae in the head with a pistol. Zae screamed out in pain grabbing his head. I quickly got up, ran, and locked myself in the bathroom. The bed sheet still wrapped around my body.

"My bitch, really nigga, what the fuck is wrong with you?" Vega punched him in the face. They must've heard the sounds coming from the bedroom when they entered the house, whatever the case, I was glad to see them.

"What the fuck mane?" Zae cried

"You gone rape her in my house on my fucking bed?" He kicked Zae.

"I'm sorry mane, I didn't know you gave a fuck about her like that, I'm sorry." he pleaded.

"So, you mean to tell me, all the year's you've known me, have you ever saw a bitch in my house besides Princess?" He pointed at Princess who was grinning and twirling her gun. Zae knew he had crossed the line. He knew at any moment Princess was gonna put a bullet in his head.

"HAVE YOU NIGGA." Vega yelled.

"No." Zae said like a little boy.

"NO, that's right nigga you haven't, not even MY FUCKING MOMMA." He punched him again

"I, I, I'm," Zae stuttered

"SORRY nigga you already said that shit. I save yo ass time after time and you always doing some stupid shit. Now this, you rape my girl!" Vega yelled.

Zae could tell there was no reasoning with Vega. It would not be easy to talk his way out of this. Defeated, he still tried once more to plea with Vega. "Vega please, not over no female; I swear I didn't know. I love you bruh. I'll never disrespect you like that again. I promise." Vega did have a soft spot for Zae, that's why a lot a niggas let Zae make it, but without a blink, he gave Princess the order. She put a bullet through his skull, sending him back to his maker.

"SHYNE"

The gunshot had me frozen solid. I couldn't move as I heard footsteps approaching the door and twisting the knob.

"Pepa" Vega shouted. I still couldn't move. "It's ok, open the door ma." He was twisting the knob.

I unlocked the door still shaking. I flew into Vega's arm he held me tight I could see Princess dragging Zae's dead body out of the room. I closed my eyes again to get rid of the image. "I got you ma, I'm sorry, I'll never let shit happen to you like that again. You got my word. Let's get up out of here for tonight." He cradled me in his arms like a baby. That night we checked into a hotel. While Capone and Princess watched over the cleanup crew that cleaned Vega's room. My mind was all over the place. I especially felt bad for Tameka.

That's the reason she been so distant. I could only imagine what she went through that night, and it still doesn't explain why she didn't say shit.

"Did you know" I asked Vega. "Did I know what?" he looked suspect. "That he raped Tameka." I said

"SHYNE"

"He always doing dumb shit. He told me he gave her some guap, so I knew his dumb as did something stupid." Vega said nonchalantly.

"Money! how much.?" I was mad as hell. No amount of money is worth her silence from me.

"I don't know ma, maybe 5 or 8 racks" he shrugged his shoulders. I didn't want to believe it. Tameka wouldn't keep nothing from me. I can understand why. I'll call her later, right then all I wanted was Vega. His security and his coke. $$$$$$$$$$$$$$$$$$$$$$$$$$$$$$$$$$$$$

"What's going on lady?" I gave Tameka a hug as I walked into her house.

"Nothing much love, I see life been good to you, ya blinging." She grabs my wrist

"Bitch is that a cartier?" She gasped. I shook my head

"yes." I smiled "I guess he treating you good, huh?" she said,

"You know me." I shrug my shoulders.

"I do bitch and ever since you got with Vega, your ass ain't been home much." She said

KARMA

"SHYNE"

"I like him an all, but I still got a feeling he's not who he says he is. He's like this mysterious person." I think that was what kept me drawn to him. The unfamiliar and his thuggish bad boy image, but I wasn't there to talk about Vega.

"Where's James?" I looked around not wanting to say nothing if he was in the house.

"Him and Jamie at the mall" she said,

"You remember Zae right Vega's homeboy?" I asked and watched her whole demeanor change.

"Yea." She said not looking at me.

"He's dead." I tried to search her face for emotions, but she learned her poker face from the best (me).

"Really what happened?" she asked, "Vega killed him." I said,

"Why the hell would Vega kill his boy?" she asked,

"He raped me." I explained

"OMG Pepa, I'm so sorry." She grab my hand.

"SHYNE"

"I should've warned you about him." She began to cry. "What do you mean?" I played dumb. She took a deep breath.

"That night at Vega's house he raped me too. Saying that's what I come for, that's what I wanted. He made me feel like shit. He was biting me and shit. I couldn't even have sex with James for like weeks from the way he disrespected my body." She paused "I'm glad he's dead." You could feel the rage in her voice, almost scary. "I've never been through no shit like that in my life. All I could think about was James and Jamie. How I was so stupid for being out of town with a nigga. That nigga could've killed me and threw my body in the Chattahoochee fucking punk." She spat

I felt bad for Tameka I think she got it way worst then me. "That's why I been to myself. Spending time with my family. James been asking me to marry him. I think it's time. I love him. I don't know what I would do without him." She said honestly

"I say its past time you marry James. I'm so happy for you." I gave her a big hug.

KARMA

"SHYNE"

"I wish the same happiness for you friend."
She smiles at me.

"One day, one day but do me a favor." I
said, "What's that?" she asked,

"Don't ever be ashamed to tell me
anything, you been my girl since 4th grade." I told
her

"I know and I'm sorry I felt so dirty,
especially when he threw money at me, I guess so
I wouldn't talk." She said near tears

"Are you serious?" I acted surprised

"Seven thousand, I felt even worse. Don't
get me wrong, I've had sex with niggas for a lot
less, but that fucking creep never." She spat. "I
understand Meek" I hugged her.

"I love you." She said, "I love you more." I
left Tameka's house headed to see my mother at
her office. She says its urgent.

I don't know what she does or why she
needs an office at the law firm. She was just the
man's assistant, and since they been married, she
half ass does that, but if I know my mother and I
do know my mother, she would rather hold down

the position than let some other woman sneak in like she did.

I waved at John as I walked pass his door. John was a 32-year-old white nice-looking man. He worked at the firm the past 8 years since he gotten out of law school. Pretty good lawyer too and made real good money. He loves young black girls like myself. I hit him off twice, but he was way too clingy. He closed his door as soon as he saw my face. I laughed knowing he hates my guts. I guess he thought I was marriage material, silly him. Every time I come by the office; I make sure to wear something extra tight to tease his corny ass.

"Hey ma you wanted to see me?" I asked. She raised up from her oversized office chair and gave me a big bear hug like we were the perfect mother and daughter team. "This gotta be about some money, who's dead now." I thought to myself.

"Hey baby have a seat" she escorted me over to the plush sitting chairs in her office. "I got good news. I talked with Christopher and he said with your permission, we can get your money from that money-grubbing ass Terri." My mother said. I knew it! We hardly talked about anything but money.

"Ma Terri isn't holding my money." I explained

"I bet it was all her idea in the first place. 25 my ass, who does he think he is, sounds like her money hungry ass. You know that's the only reason she married your father." She said. "Ain't that the pot calling the kettle." I thought to myself. "Momma I'll get the money" she interrupted me.

"I know all that but, we can get it now for you, of course. That low down piece of shit father of yours---" I interrupted her.

"Mama stop it." I shouted, "Just cut the shit." The words
slipped out before I knew it. She was getting on my nerves.

"You better watch your fucking mouth little girl." She said threw clinched teeth looking around making sure no one else could hear us. I rolled my eyes. I'd heard enough.

"SHYNE"

"I'm out ma. I gotta go." I stood to leave. "Go ahead, be a fool all your life. Let people walk all over you. I'm your mother. I got your best interest at heart." She pointed at herself. "You mean your best interest."

"You got some fucking balls." She was right, I was testing her. I knew at any moment she could back hand me. I didn't care at that point.

"You think I need your little money." She got up in my face. "No, you don't, but you still want it. I'm not bothered by that money ma. It's not going any anywhere, so please let it go." She was pissed. I thought I saw the devil rise up off her shoulders.

"Ok, whatever you say." She went back to her seat behind her desk and pretend to do paperwork. "Bye ma." I said. She waved me off, not even looking up. I didn't care I was in a hurry to get out of her presences.

I thought about Vega on my way to the house. Was it him or did I just want to get high every time he crossed my mind, so did the coke? What was I doing Vega was dangerous and I knew this. I had plenty opportunity to leave him alone. I

"SHYNE"

jumped in the shower as soon as I came home and got into something comfortable. My phone starts to vibrate in my purse.

"Hello" I answered.

"You miss me," Sexy male voice.

"Who is this?" I joked.

"Girl stop it, you know you been waiting by the phone for me to call." He joked

"Well, I was just thinking about you." I flopped down on my sofa. "Really." He said,

"What you want to do about it?" he asked. I been with him so much lately, I felt as if I was neglecting my own residence. I didn't want to get to attached to Vega, so I lied.

"I got a lot going on this week. Can I hit you up next weekend?" I asked

"Nope." I just smiled. "No" I said.

"Open your door." Ain't no way, I thought to myself, as I ran to open my door.

"What up ma?" he stood in the doorway looking good as ever. I gave him a big bear hug. I missed everything about him, his smile, his touch, and his smell. It was now safe to say I was deep in love with Vega.

"SHYNE"

"How you know where I stay?" I asked. "You think I been kicking it with you all this time and I don't know where you live. I had you checked out." He said seriously. I didn't know whether
to be happy or afraid. "Nice little cozy place you got here. How do you afford such exquisite taste?" He said holding up the $100 picture frame with a picture of my father holding me as a newborn.

"I got my ways." I said

"Really." He took me into his arms. "I love you." His words caught me off guard. What was this man trying to do to me?

"Do you really?" I couldn't make myself say the words, no matter how I felt about him.

"So, you don't love me." He asked again, I didn't know what to say. "Of course." He grabs my hand.
"Let's go." He never asks me, just gives orders. "Where we going?" I asked like it really mattered. I knew I was going with him. "Vegas,"

"Las Vegas," I said like really. "Unless you know of another Vegas." He joked "Ok let me grab somethings." I tried to go to my closet.

"SHYNE"

"No, you don't need anything. You with me. I told you I got you." He led me out the door. I only had time to grab my Jimmy Choo purse and Prada sunglasses. I had on a grey BeBe tank top, and blue jeans. My hair was in an untamed ponytail. I looked a hot mess as we boarded the private jet. If I hadn't already been impressed, I was now this shit was dope. Food, drinks, tv, and a bed, it was like a movie scene for real. I was living someone else life to the fullest.

I called my aunt as soon as we got settled in the Palms Resort Hotel. Of course, she told me to be careful and send her lots of pictures. She was upset with me for cursing at my mom, but she understood. I Should've known she would call her and play the victim. Now it was time to relax.

"It's beautiful." I admired the view from the top floor. I could see all of Vegas. We had two balcony double doors lead in the bedrooms. There were bottles of champagne in ice buckets, and butterflies were decorated in bottom of pool and on the walls. When I stepped outside the balcony, it was a pool on the other side.

"SHYNE"

Vega handed me 2 stacks of money from his briefcase. 10,000 bands wrapped around them.

"Go down to the beauty salon and then go shopping." He demanded. "I could get use to this." I thought.

"Where are we going." I asked so I could know what to buy.

"It's Vegas baby! We here to play! First, we will go down to the casino, then later to the MGM Grand to watch the fight." He said

"Mayweather," I saw him on all the billboards since we landed.

"Of course." He said. Now I can say it. I'm in love!

Mayweather was the hottest boxer on the rise. Tonight, I would be watching him live and up close. My first time in Vegas! My first fight! "I love you! I love you!" I threw my arms around him. "I love you too, this is nothing baby. I'll make all your dreams come true." he kissed me softly on my lips.

"I'll see ya when I get back." I said. Then I exit the room with Vega's 20,000 dollars in my purse. I quickly went down to the floors with the shopping plaza. Hotels with shopping stores were new to me. I couldn't wait to call Tameka.

"Girl guess where I'm at?" I said excited
"Ain't no telling, you never at home. Where you at bitch?" she asked

"Vegas." I told her

"No shit." she said,

"I'm on my way shopping so I can get something to wear to the fight tonight." I explained

"Mayweather?" she asked

"Um huh. This nigga let me loose with 20 bands bitch. I'm about to cope you everything I buy me, so clear out some closet space," I told her dead serious. She was excited and happy for me.

"Well James ordered the fight so I'm a be looking for your ass. Let me know what you wear so I can spot ya." She said excited!

"I'll text you when I get dressed." I assured her. "Bye girl, be careful." She hung up.

I found a long sleeve, tight fitting black Chanel dress with white Chanel signs all over it. I also found some black Chanel heals with the silver

"SHYNE"

Chanel buckle on top to match. I coped Tameka one too in white. My hair was pulled up in a long high ponytail. I had to be on point. Tonight, I was going after Mayweather himself.

On my way back to the hotel room, as soon as I got off the elevator, I passed by Princess who gave me a quick nod and kept on walking. How and why is she here I thought to myself.

"What up ma, your hair looks really nice," Vega was putting on his tailor-made Tom Ford suit. "Water still hot, we better get to moving. I got a car coming to pick us up in 2 hours. That's it that's all you got." Vega joking about me always taking forever to get dressed. I didn't even blink.

"What's Princess doing here?" I asked. Vega fixing his tie not looking at me.

"She's like my American express, I never leave home without her. He smiled as if I was joking.

"What, you don't like princess?" he asked me as if I was a child. I'm not the jealous type, I just like to know what I'm dealing with and make sure this hoe doesn't snipe me in my sleep. I get nothing but weird vibes when she's around. "Trust me ma, don't be jealous, she's necessary for business, that's it." He planted a wet kiss on my lips. "Now get dressed." He said.

I really didn't know or care what Princess job was anymore. If he's fucking her, it would come out sooner or later. I'm in Vegas, the city that never sleeps, it's time to turn up the heat. So, fuck Princess.

"Did you bring the stuff?" I was too ashamed to call it what it was cocaine. I didn't want to admit, I was a drug addict. The kind of people I once looked down on for doing drugs. "You think I boarded a plane with coke." Vega smiled at me. Now I was disappointed, I wanted to get high.

"I guess not." I said softly.

"I had Princess to drop it off." He was trying to read me.

"You want a bite to eat first. I had Princess bring some take out also." He said "Eat." Fuck that, we just ate on the damn plane. I want to get high, and I wanted to get high now.

"SHYNE"

The mere fact that I knew the coke was so close made my whole night change. I couldn't think of anything else at the moment.

"I just needed a little bit to loosen me up. I'm still a little off from the plane ride." I told him Somehow my poker face was not working. Vega could see straight through me. I felt ashamed, I felt bad, but not bad enough for me not want to get high. He hesitated but soon gave in. My eyes lit up like a kid at Christmas when I saw the bag filled with white powder.

"Here you go." He threw the bag on the table with an attitude.

"What's wrong?" I asked because his energy had seriously changed.

"You." He pointed at me.

"Me, what the hell you mean?" I said surprised "Look at yourself, you turning into a real junkie, don't want to eat just get high." He said. Ok now, I'm really confused. It's his fault he offered me this shit in the first place.

"Ok I'm sorry, your right let's eat." I said not wanting him to be mad at me. "I'm not hungry anymore." He said. "Good let's get high." I said to myself.

He took off his jacket and threw it on the back of the chair. His whole facial expression changed as he took the bag of coke and dipped his pinky in it. I didn't know what to do or say. He got up mumbling something to himself. He came back with a plate and poured out a pile of coke and handed it to me. I sat still. I didn't know whether to take it or not.

"TAKE IT." He shouted. "You know you want the shit, it's the whole reason you with me." He jumped up mumbling again. "Junkie, money hungry, ass bitches." He kept saying over and over. He started pacing the floor like a lunatic. I was ready to get the fuck out of there, Vega had lost his mind talking to me crazy. I'm not a junkie and that's exactly what I told his ass.

"I know good damn well you ain't talking to me. I'm here because I want to be. I don't need yo ass for shit. I been doing this shit. I did---" my words muffled by a slap to my face. Now I've seen people fly across the room on TV but you could've never told me that shit happens in real life. He hit

"SHYNE"

me so hard, I landed in the kitchen. I immediately grab my face which was starting to swell.

"What BITCH?" he yelled. I was still dazed as he charged towards me. He slapped me again. He picked me up by my throat squeezing it as I clawed at his big hands trying to pry them from my throat. "Say something else bitch. Don't ever talk to me like that. Who the fuck you think you are? I've killed niggas for less disrespect. You hear me? I'll fuck you up in this mother fucker. You hear me?" He yelled shaking my body as if I weighed 3 pounds. I struggled to loosen his grip, tears rolling down my check as no more oxygen could get to my brain. Once again, I was in a situation I couldn't control. My life was in his hands I thought to myself as the room went black.

I had no idea how long I'd been out, maybe two or three mins, or maybe an hour. I could hear sounds in the room, but they were really low like my hearing had left my body. I woke up on the kitchen floor, confused at first, then I quickly remembered. I was pissed that this nigga I'd fallen for had actually left me on the floor like I was nothing to him.

"SHYNE"

I saw Vega sitting on the sofa watching the fight on TV, a plate of cocaine keeping him company. His shirt was off, all he had on were slacks and a wife beater. My body ached as I pick myself up off the floor making all the noise I possibly could to draw his attention. He never even turned around. I walked over to the sofa to take the seat next to him. I was scared to open my mouth to say anything to him. I saw my phone blinking with a message from Tameka (Where you at girl? What you got on? I told everyone. We looking for you on TV wave or something bitch.)

I didn't respond back, I wanted to cry. I couldn't let her know that I wasn't at the fight. That me and Vega had a fight and he chocked me unconscious.

Vega just stared at me for what felt like hours. I felt like a little girl. I knew he was disappointed in me. He walked into the bedroom and closed the door leaving me alone with my thoughts and the plate of cocaine. I tried not to look at it. Telling myself I had self-control. I couldn't stop thinking about the feeling it gave me and how I needed to escape reality right now.

"SHYNE"

I was smart enough to know that it was only temporarily, but I did care. I wanted to feel that tingle again, that numbness. I wasn't a junkie, like Vega thinks I am. Maybe I'll take the plate in the kitchen. Get it away from me. I took the plate and placed it on the kitchen counter and went back into the living room to watch Mayweather. I looked back at the plate then the TV.

"Shit" I said aloud. I wonder was he doing this on purpose. Probably standing on the other side of the door waiting on me to take one hit, so he could be right, so he could say I was a junkie and using him for his coke. Was this his plan all alone to get me hooked on coke. How many women has he done this too before me? All the wining and dining, unlimited shopping sprees, 100,000 dollars hotel rooms, this is what he wanted. He wanted to be able to control me. All of a sudden, it made sense, maybe I had been the one who'd gotten tricked, maybe I was being played.

How I'd gotten so close to the plate, I don't remember. I placed the bill in my hand, closed my left nostril, and snorted really hard.

"SHYNE"

I went back to the sofa, paranoid that Vega was watching me and would bust out the room at any moment. I was paranoid as hell. I kept walking back and forth from the sofa to the closed door trying to listening for any sound. "1,2,3,4, it's over. It's over. Mayweather wins again." I heard the commentator say.

This calls for a celebration. I was super high by now. Hitting line after line, all my troubles faded away. I had not a care in the world, only a feeling was running like an electric shock through my veins. I watched the celebration on TV and felt as if I was really there with them. My body was starting to get numb. The coke was doing what it normally does, makes me horny. I twisted the knob on the door. It was locked.

"Stupid ass" I threw up my middle finger as I walked away from the door. There was no way I was about to beg for no dick. I snorted another line of coke. I started dancing around with the plate in my hand. I was high as an eagle's pussy and I didn't want to come down. I could see the sunlight peeping in. OMG, I hadn't even been to sleep. I'd been up all night getting high and I still wasn't sleepy and now I had a problem, my plate was now empty. I needed more and knew just how to get it.

"Open this door," I was beating the door with all my might. I grew the balls from somewhere I couldn't be thinking straight. This nigga just chocked me last night and left me unconscious on the floor for ain't no telling how long.

"Open the fucking door Vega." I continued. He snatched the door opened the scene must've caught him off guard I was standing there butt naked and high out my mind.

"What the fuck girl." He snapped

"I'm sleepy" I said because I couldn't remember what I wanted "Then why the fuck you ain't sleep then." He asked I didn't say anything "Look girl find you something safe to do, stop playing with me. Don't make me kill yo ass. We the only people on this floor I promise wont nobody hear you scream." He warned

I visioned Princess dragging my body out like she did Zae's and I straighten up really quick.

"SHYNE"

"I'm not playing." I said he knew exactly what was wrong with me. He probably left the shit there in the first place.

"What you want pepa?" He pushed past me and saw the empty plate. If looks could kill I would have feel six feet under.

"Oh, I see, you snorted up a whole plate of coke" he grab the plate and threw it into the wall. It shattered I damn near jumped out my skin. I was afraid and confused all over again. Terrified he would choke me again and this time I may not wake up. I began to cry. I cried hard and loud falling to the floor. I guess I played on his sensitive side finally. He came to my rescue he let out a puff of air rubbed his head in frustration

"Ok baby, stop it stop crying I'm sorry." He picked me up kissing my bruised face. I could tell in his eyes he meant it he was really sorry for putting his hands on me. Or maybe that's what I wanted to believe.

"I'm sorry ma, come on let's get you in bed." He said leading me to the bedroom.it had to been 7am. I hadn't had any sleep all night my body was tired but my brain was wide awake and I was still horny. I wanted to be fucked like only he could fuck me. I stopped walking he looked at me as if something were wrong. "I don't want to sleep; I want a nut." I told him

Vega smiled, he knew the cocaine made me real freaky and I was gonna get a nut with or without him. He definitely didn't want to miss this ride "Come get it" he said.

$$$$$$$$$$$$$$$$$$$$$$$$$$$$$$

Two months pasted since the Vegas incident. I hadn't been home. I told my aunt I would be attending school at the university of Memphis this fall so she wouldn't ask to many questions. Vega still paid my rent at my apartment in case I wanted to go back home. My mother still wasn't talking to me, but she would come around eventually she always does.

Things were good between me and Vega for the moment, I mean we would still argue and he would still knock the hell out of me if he didn't like what came out of my mouth. He was gone on a run to Miami. Check things out since he had to put someone else in Zae spot. I didn't want to stay in the big house so I stay at the other house.

"SHYNE"

"Hi Capone." I let him into the house to pick up his package that Vega had left him. He was dressed in Ed Hardy shirt and shorts he wore a white durag underneath his Ed Hardy hat.

"Sup" he said as he closed the door behind him. We had basically became like family. They were the people I spent most of my time with. I noticed him stare at my bruise on my jaw.

"What happened to your face?" he asked as he turned my head to the side to get a better look

"Nothing" I lied he just looked as if he felt sorry for me.

"You don't gotta save face for me. I don't get in V business, but I gotta ask why to go through shit you don't have to go through. Why not just go home?" he asked

I wondered the same thing almost every night why am I still here. I had plenty of money. I didn't need Vega anymore. I was in love and love loves nobody. Plus, Vega wasn't always mean sometimes he was the sweetest person ever. "Why would I do that?" I answered embarrassed "I like being here." I said

"SHYNE"

"I guess you right, but you too pretty to let a nigga hit on you. V my nigga but I ain't neva been with putting my hands on a female. If I gotta put my hands on ya I don't need ya." He said

"It's not what it seems," I had no comeback for his words, I knew I couldn't have been the first women that Vega took through this probably wouldn't be the last. "You know what you like." He shrugged his shoulder

I walked to the back to get his drugs I could feel his eyes glued on my ass, something no man could resist. I gave him the 18 kilos in a duffle bag. "Thanks shorty. If you need something let me know." He handed me his card "Are you giving me your number?" I took the card harmlessly flirting

"Nawl it ain't that type of party shorty. Just know V out of town. Just lending a helping hand." He smiled "Just wondering." I heard shouting outside "What the hell?" We both ran to the door

"Where is V's black ass?" A light skin chic with a bad weave was yelling

"SHYNE"

"Mane V ain't here and don't bring all that drama around today." Capone must know the chic, I figured she was one of Vega's side hoe's

"Get the fuck back Capone, my fucking car note ain't been paid, and he not answering the phone. He got me all the way fucked up." She said pointing to her c class Mercedes. She saw me in the doorway.

"Who the fuck is that?" she asked Capone

"Get back in your car Bree." He walked towards her like he was trying to protect me. Tuh don't let this pretty face fool ya I been fighting hoes all my life like Sophia, and she want be no different.

"You know Vega ain't having this shit at his house." He said

"Oh, hell nawl, that better be one of your bitches, my car bout to be repossessed and this nigga got to nerve to have a bitch laying up in his house. Is tha bitch with you or him. You know what it don't matter." She pulled out her phone I guess to call Vega I don't know, and I didn't care the bitch had violated. Nobody talks crazy to Pep nobody.

KARMA

"SHYNE"

I walked onto the porch so she could get a better look. That really made her go off especially since Capone wouldn't say I was with him. She knew I was there for Vega. There it is again the bitch word I knew I was gonna have to whoop this hoe.

"Bitch, yo momma a bitch." I yelled She threw her phone down then charged towards me. Of course, Capone grabs her but not before she swings and hits me in the face, now it's on. I tried to take that bitch head off, Capone still between us, I hit is ass too. Should've gotten out my way.

He managed to get her in the car, but she busted out the passenger door and we locked up again. he pulled us apart throwing me back in the house, guarding the front door.

"Calm down you don't want no laws around here. Did you forget the dope was in the house?" He was right I wasn't thinking I was like a raging bull pacing back and forth

"You cool?" he said still guarding the door   I didn't say a word I was too pissed. I heard the sound of glass shattering.

KARMA

"SHYNE"

"Don't move." He pointed his finger at me like a child. I heard tire screeching and a horn blowing "Fuck" he ran back in the house

"Did that bitch just—" he interrupted me "Don't worry about it, I'm a call my homeboy to fix your windshield." He said,

"I got a hair appointment at 3:00, I need my car." I was mad as hell

"I'll take you, come on." I didn't know how I felt about him driving me around town. My hair was in an emergency state though. "No that's ok. I don't want to bother you. I know you got more important shit to do I'll call for a car." I said,

"It's no trouble I promise." He insisted "Let me get my bag." I grabbed my Birkin bag

He dropped me off at the salon and 3 hours later he picked me up and paid $250 for my hair. That didn't bother me men always paid for things for me

"You look nice." He said smiling

"I look nice or my hair look nice." I said,

"Yea that too." He smiled

"Thank you." I smiled I couldn't tell if he was flirting with me or not

"SHYNE"

"I talked to V he said he will handle Bree." He told me

"He better or I will, I mean I'm no hater, if Vega paying her bills so be it. Don't bring that shit to me." I said with an attitude he laughed at me "So, you cool with him paying her bills." He said smiling

"What I don't know want hurt me. It's a way to do everything ya feel me. I know what kind of nigga I'm dealing with. I know he got other women I'm not naive." I rolled my eyes "I hear that." He said

Why did he have to be so damn sexy, why was I acting thirsty. I shouldn't have been looking at him at all. Maybe I was just missing Vega.

"You got women?" I really wanted to know for my own personal reasons

"Is that a come on?" He looked at me funny now I hated I ever asked,

"No just asking, I never see you with a girl that's all." I told him

"You probably never will." he said,

"You gay." I asked knowing the answer He shot me daggers.

"SHYNE"

"Nawl I just don't got time for drama. Like that shit back at V house, that I almost got my ass kicked about. No, I'll stay married to the money." He smiled.

"Meeee Too." We both laughed.

Capone was cool as shit. Somebody I could really get use too. He was charming I knew he was a bad boy, but he hid it well which also made him dangerous in my book "You hungry" he asked "Yes. I'm always hungry" I answered he laughed "Where you want to eat?" he asked "Crumpy's they have the best wings in town." I answered "Crumpy's it is." He said

We went to get my food then he dropped me off at the house. I noticed my windshield was fixed.

"That was quick." I said,

"I told you I got you." He said Scared of what that might meant so I quickly got out the car.

"You gonna be straight here, you don't need me to take you out to the big house, do you?" he asked concerned as if I couldn't drive myself

"SHYNE"

"No, I'm good thanks again." I said before walking into the house

I tried to call Vega his phone went to voicemail. I'm sure he got some chic with him. I ate my food and fell asleep,

I could hear my phone ringing in my sleep.

"Hello" I answered my voice groggy

"Damn you sound like a nigga." Vega said "Whatever, I was sleep what time is it?" I asked

"3:48" he answered

"A.M., you better try again, good night." I teased knowing I wanted to hear his voice

"Girl stop playing. I miss you. You don't miss me?" he asked,

"You know I do your girl stopped by." I felt the need to throw that in there

"That ain't my girl, I only got one girl and that's you. I'll be home in a couple days." he promised

"Well, you need to handle your business better than what you been doing." I said,

"Don't stress ma, I got me, and I got you too." He assured me

KARMA

"SHYNE"

"I'm not stressing I can handle mine." He laughed

"I heard about ya," he said,

"You got something for me?" I asked,

"You know I do." He answered,

"Can't wait to see you." I said,

"I'll be home soon ma get some sleep; I love you." "Love you too." I hung up

I placed my phone in my bag. And pulled out my stash. That I now kept with me in my lipgloss container. I took me a quick bump to wake me on up. I did coke on the regular now. I mean I could quit if I wanted to that was the difference between me and a junkie, I choose to get high I loved the feeling the coke gave me I still looked good still had weight on me I still stayed fly so no harm done.

I could hear Vega's dogs barking in the back yard, and what sound like the garbage can tumbling. I couldn't tell if I was spooked, but what I did know was that those dogs didn't bark unless someone they didn't know was in the yard. I got my phone out. Wasn't no need in calling Vega back. He was 1000 miles away with his head buried in pussy. I got out the card that Capone gave earlier

"Hello" he answered. Thank God he was woke

"Hey its Pepa. I think someone is trying to break in." I kept starring at the front door paranoid

"I doubt if anyone's that stupid, but I'm a swing by anyway I'm not that far out. I'll be there in 20 minutes." He hung up

I was terrified I started watching the clock. I threw the rest of the coke back in my bag, I didn't want anymore. I tried my best to sober up getting impatient waiting on Capone 10 minutes had pasted. "Fuck this." I grabbed my keys and headed for my car. I had on nothing but a head wrap a black spaghetti strap top white boy shorts and black converse.

When I opened my car door. I looked around and didn't see anyone. Thinking I was tripping I closed the car door to go back inside. That's when the bag came over my head. I tried to scream then I felt a hand over my mouth. Once again, I'm in a situation I can't control. I struggled to get the bag from over my head. The bag got tighter suffocating the air in my lung.

"Shut the fuck up bitch or you die." He snatched the bag off my face. I fell to the ground gasping for air. A gun was quickly placed to my head. He drags me by my hair covering my mouth.

"Where is the dope?" he asked I pointed to the house I wasn't about to die over no dope. Vega had plenty. I never been so scared in my life.

"This is how its gonna work." He stuck the gun in my mouth "We are going in together, you gonna give me the dope and I'll let you live ok." He said

I shook my head all I could see was his eyes the black ski mask hid his face. He pushed me in the back with the gun that was my que to start walking. I thought about the time I was raped by Zae and Vega saved me. I'd cheated death one to many times. I didn't think it would happen again. I knew as soon as I gave him what he wanted; he would probably kill me. He threw my body into the porch steps as he took off running, I didn't

"SHYNE"

know what had happened, but I was glad. My body hurt as I raised up to see Capone's headlights.

"Thank God." I said as I saw Capone jump out his truck with a pistol in his hand. I fainted

"Pepa Pep wake up." I could hear him saying, I felt dizzy as hell

"You ok do I need me to call an ambulance?" he asked me placing me in his truck.

"No, I'm fine." I answered,

"What happened?" he asked,

"He ran off he tried to rob me he wanted the dope." I said still shaking "I thought he was gonna kill me." I started crying. He put his arms around me and held me tight

"It's ok you safe now, don't cry I want let shit happen to you." He pulled out his phone to call Vega and give him the run down. He told him he was taking me home. Home that's funny I really need to take my ass home before I ended up dead.

"Did you see how the nigga looked?" he asked I shook my head no he just stared feeling sorry for me

"SHYNE"

"What a day huh?" he said sarcastically I didn't respond. I knew he just wanted to help but all I could think about was calling my aunt and telling her the truth, I wasn't in school I had fucked up my life, I'm on drugs and, in a relationship with a king pin that slaps me around a little. Please come and get me

"You ok?" Capone ask breaking my thoughts

"No" I really wasn't

"Come on I got you." We walked into the house "You know you safe here, don't nobody know about this house but a few people." He said

"I know but I hate being at this house by myself. I just don't like it." I said. He looked confused so I asked him

"Can you stay for a while please?" I asked I was shook up and I didn't want to be alone

"I'll take the couch" he said I didn't give a damn if he slept outside in his car as long as he was close

"You want a drink?" I asked,

"SHYNE"

"I don't drink." He said like I should know
"Really. Hell, I thought everybody got drunk" I said

"Yeah, really." He smiled
"Then what do you do?" Wanting to know his poison

"Why I got to do something. Why I just can't be about my money. I need a leveled head at all times. Drugs and alcohol clouds your judgement, but of course you know that" he winked

"Smart ass, I guess you right. I just didn't know you were so damn corny that's all." We both laughed. I wanted to know who was April, the girl he had tatted on his neck since he doesn't do relationship.

"You must've loved her?" I asked about the tattoo "To death, this my sister she was murdered a couple years back."

"I'm sorry to hear that, my dad just died so I feel your pain." I poured me a glass of grey goose

I turned on the TV to find us a movie. I was no longer sleepy we watched Tyler perry's The

"SHYNE"

Family That Preys. Then I gave Capone a blanket to sleep under.

"Thanks" he grabs the banket and took off his chain and shirt, so he could be more comfortable. I didn't know if he should stay anymore., as I watched his biceps bulging out from his white tee I started to sweat. I needed to get the hell up to my room, and fast I turned to leave "Where you going?" he looked confused "To bed." I lied

"Nigga you ain't sleepy." He was right "A lot done went on today my body bout to shut down." Making excuses

"You don't got to worry about that you safe now. I promise a mother fucker gone answer for putting they hands on you." I could tell he meant just that

"Thanks for everything today, I don't know what would have happened if you hadn't shown up when u did." I said. "Come on shorty, put another one of those corny ass movies on." He said

I smiled and took the seat beside him. I cover up with my throw keeping enough space in between us. We must've fallen asleep watching the movie. I woke up around 7am I glanced over at him sleeping so peacefully. I wonder what would he do if I kissed his lips. Would he tell Vega would Vega believe him? I placed my hands underneath his shirt rubbing on his abs, watching his facial expression. I had all the opportunity to stop, no damage had been done yet he wasn't even awake. But I didn't want too. I lightly unbuckled his pants. I knew when he popped his eyes open to see me his head might be a little fucked up, so to save me the embarrassment I needed his dick to be hard. That's the only brain he needed to be thinking with I pulled it out a stroked it slowly until it was at full salute.

"What the fuck you doing?" He asked me, but yet he didn't try to stop me. I didn't know what to say so I kissed his lips. I wanted him I didn't care that I had crossed the line, there was no turning back now. He pushed me back looking dead into my eyes

"You sure you want to go there?" The look in his eyes let me know the decision was on me. I took off his tank and placed my lips on his chest.

"SHYNE"

The sound's he were making let me know to keep going. He palmed my breast I took off my shirt and bra so he could get a better feel. He dropped his pants now his dick wasn't as big as Vega's of course but it was nice. I wondered did he know what to do with it. He lay me on the Persian rug and placed his mouth on my most precious possession. I couldn't help but scream it felt so good as he teased my nipples with his fingers. He picked me up in the air my legs on his shoulders while he eats me out. I beg him to stop I had already cum. I wanted him inside me. He took me off his shoulders. Placing me against the wall, with each stoke I could feel every vein every muscle as he fucked me long and hard.

"You want to cum" he kissed me in the mouth. "Cum how many times." I thought to myself. "Yes baby, Yes." I said as we both released ourselves. We both were speechless after the feeling was gone. Now our thoughts were going did we regret it. Could we trust one another, Vega would kill us both. I didn't know what I felt. All I knew is I was digging deeper and deeper. Could I trust him, hell could I trust me? I lay in his arms I felt safe. I wanted to be able to trust him I needed to be able to trust him.

Vega called around noon

"Hello" I looked over at Capone asleep "What's good Ma" he said,

"It's all good when you coming home?" I asked hoping he may be close. I hated to admit it, but I was missing him "A couple more days" He answered This nigga playing fo'real

"Nigga you said a couple days a couple days ago. You been gone a week tomorrow." I woke Capone up with my yelling

"I know ma, but shit got fucked up down here. I promise I'll be home soon." He assured me "Do you even care I could've been killed last night?" I asked him I was upset that he wasn't rushing to my aid.

"Come on ma you know I care about you. You my world. I already put the word out. The mother fucker that put their hands on you is a dead man walking." He threatens I loved to hear Vega talk like that all that gangster shit turned me on

"SHYNE"

"I'm sorry bae I can be a brat sometimes. It's just I don't want to stay in this big ass house by myself." I told him thinking he would hurry home.

"You right I'm a call Twain, nawl I'm a call Capone have him keep an eye on you until I get back." He told me

"Capone" I almost shitted Capone saw the look in my eyes like a dear caught in head lights. "What?" he mouthed impatiently "I don't need a babysitter." Especially not him

"I'm a call him now." Ignoring my comments. I could also hear a female voice in the background "Who is that?" I asked "Princess" he answered but I knew he was lying I just hung up the phone I didn't have the energy. "Fuck Vega".

"What he says?" Capone motioning with his hands before I could answer his phone rang. He talked to Vega for 10 minutes outside before walking back towards me.
"I guess it's me and you." He smiled

"You don't gotta do this I'll go to a hotel for a couple days." I really didn't feel like being there, if it weren't the middle of the week, I would've went home but everyone thought I was in class during the week so I couldn't go there.

"I gave V my word, so we stuck together." He said "Whatever." I threw my hands up walking upstairs to take a shower. The shower helped me clear my head. I needed to get high, but I didn't want Capone judging me. I thought about how Vega was playing me. I thought about my father and I wished he were here. It's funny how when people gone you miss them the most. I was really being selfish, just wanting shit to go my way.

Capone was standing in the doorway as I stepped out the shower. "What?" I said with an attitude as I walked past him naked, I felt no need to cover my body since he had already seen the goods.

"What's up shorty your whole attitude changed after you talked to V." he was right I was taking my stress for Vega out on him and he was only trying to help

"Sorry I'm bugging" I was sincere

"It's cool. SOOO do we pretend last night didn't happen?" He asked

"SHYNE"

I was used to pretending like nothing happen sex was just that. The nigga did fuck me to sleep I can't lie, but I didn't trust men. Just like now Vega's cheating ass laid up with God knows who. I walked towards him still naked placing my hands around his waist and gave him a kiss on his lips. "Last night can last as long as you want it too." I teased him he pulled me in closer looking into my eyes

"You ain't gotta be hard with me. I'm not that nigga that's trying to use you or hurt you." He said sincerely

Now Capone I couldn't really read which was scary as hell because I could read anyone. He was like a sweet version of Vega.

"So, what are you saying?" I was confused "I said it." He bent down and kissed my lips. His lips were so soft I got lost in them, for a moment I thought that this was real, but I knew this could never be. He walked off leaving me to my thoughts "You fixing breakfast." He yelled from the hall

I sure am. I put on my Victoria secret charcoal grey lace panty and bra set. And went

KARMA

down to cook breakfast. He was looking at me like I'd lost my mind. "Really pep." He said "What? this is how I cook." I rolled my eyes "Naked." His eyes not focused on my face "I'm not naked." I loved teasing him. He couldn't control himself and I knew it. He came into the kitchen placing his hands on my ass. Kissing my neck. If Vega thought, he was gonna be the only one having fun. He thought wrong me, and Capone had a fuck fiesta while he was gone. On the day he returned we were as normal as a cross in church.

$$$$$$$$$$$$$$$$$$$$$$$$$$$$$$$$$$

Vega was back and life was normal again. He been buying me gifts for a month now. I think Betty wright said it best "Some gifts are guilt gifts." I was still sneaking with Capone, so I was guilty myself. Even though I had fun with Capone I'll never trade Vega for him.

"Hello." Vega took his phone in the other room, normally it didn't bother me, but I was high and he knew not to fuck with me when I'm high.

"You didn't have to walk off." I said as he walked back into our bedroom

"SHYNE"

"Man, Pepa don't start with that dumb shit. Every time you get high you on some stupid shit. Why can't you act normal?" He dipped his finger into his sac and took a hit.

"You need to stop getting high." He said I looked upside his head like I could slap him.

"Then you know not to play with me." I got real brave when I was high

"Watch yo mouth, it ain't no disrespect, I ain't talking to no female." He said

"Listen Vega I know you fuck with other women I—" he jumped up aggravated

"I'm not fucking no women. Is that all you think about, every time my phone rings it gotta be a bitch." He snapped

"You a fucking lie, I don't say shit every time yo phone ring. It's when you do that slick shit that gives yo ass away." I snapped back

"Pepa please do me a favor stop getting high." He was right there were functional addicts in the world then there was me.

"Stop being slick." I snapped

"Slick" he started laughing at me now I was really pissed

"SHYNE"

"So, you think I'm funny."

"Hilarious." He took another hit not paying me any attention

"Ok then mother fucker, what if I got on my phone and went in the back room to talk to a nigga." Yea his ass wasn't laughing now. Seeing I had his attention I went for his heart.

"That's right niggas be trying to holla at me too. What you think cause I fuck with you. I can't fuck with nobody else if I wanted too." I watched as Vega walk closer and closer, I kept right on talking never knowing when to shut my damn mouth.

"How would you like it if I was sucking—" he slaps me so hard I literally saw stars my lip split wide open as blood leak from it. I didn't understand myself why I said some of the shit I said knowing this nigga would beat me to sleep. I know I didn't like for him to hit me, but why did I feel loved when he did. I don't know, what I did know was that most time I provoked him knowing the outcome.

"SHYNE"

"Why you always got something stupid to say out your mouth, then when I hit you in that flip mother fucker, you think I did you wrong.

"Fuck you. You stupid ass bitch, you wanna suck a nigga dick go right ahead, bet he can't take care yo ass like I do." He was yelling I was still dizzy, but he had me bent

"Fuck you Vega I'm done you ain't gotta keep putting yo damn hands on me." I jumped up grabbing my purse and keys

"Where the fuck you going?" he asked I was out of there and never looking back. He had hit me for the las time I was disgusted with myself. I had dropped to a new low. No amount of money was worth the busted lips and black eyes.

"Leave bitch I don't give a fuck, and don't bring yo ass back." He yelled to my back as I drove off down the highway leaving everything behind. He could keep it. I reached in my bag and grabbed my personal stash I took a hit. Not paying attention to the cop in my rearview I swerved a little placing the stash back in my purse. That's when I saw the blue lights. "SHIT" I said aloud I just threw the dope back in my purse. Not

KARMA

knowing what to do. I had driver license so the worst thing I would get a ticket.

When his flashlight hit my eyes, he could tell I was wasted. I tried to remain calm, but I was sweating bullets I gave him my license and insurance card.

"What happen to your face?" he asked

I told him I has just got into a fight with my boyfriend and I was on my way home. Thinking I could talk my way out of him asking to search my car. I almost fainted when he asked me to step out of the car. I knew it was over as I watched him pull the coke from my purse and place me under arrest. I was taken downtown 201 popular Ave. I sat in the holding tank 5 hours before they booked me in. once again, I was in a situation beyond my control.

"What ya in for?" a white lady asked who looked like she had been arrested for prostitution

"Cocaine." I answered,

"Coke really." She said as if I was lying

"Y'all getting younger and prettier. But don't worry you'll make bond." She said I could tell it wasn't her first rodeo.

"SHYNE"

"I've never been in jail before, who do I call. How do I leave?" I asked truthfully, I just knew I wanted the hell out that box

"Where are you from? She asked

"Mississippi" I said "Hell, sweetie pie. No bondsmen is gonna wanna touch you, you from out of state. They think you may not show up for court. That you a flight risk." She said "So, what do I need to do?" I asked desperate

"Do you know anyone here who knows a bondsman who can come get you?" She asked,

"Yea I knew someone but fuck him right now." I said to myself

"Or sit here till your court date." She said, "Sit here" I pointed to the iron bench "Yep." She said

"Oh, hell no" that was out of the question as much as I hated to, I had to call Vega

"You have a collect call from" Pepa" I said into the phone. I knew no matter the argument if Vega knew I was in trouble he would come to my rescue.

"Pepa what the fuck you doing in jail." His voice with so much concern in it. I was still pissed, but he was my only option I couldn't risk anyone else knowing my bizzness. Vega was there in 30 min. The officer walked me out to the lobby. I was happy to see Vega there, he was standing there wearing a grey Ralph Lauren sweat suit and all white Airmax. He signed some papers and then we were on our way. I hated to even get in his car.

We rode to the house in silence me looking out the window the whole time. When we got to the house, he left the car running

"You can use my car for tonight. I know you said you didn't want to be here and I can't get your car till tomorrow." He walked in the house

"You damn right I ain't staying with yo bipolar ass another night." I said to myself as I walked in the house to grab some things. Mainly my other stash

"I need to grab a few things." I said but he paid me no attention, he could be a real asshole at times. I went upstairs to pack 2 suitcases I was going to a hotel for a few days give us a little space. I needed to take my ass home. I had all the opportunity that night to leave and never come back. I dragged my suitcase down the stairs being extra loud. Praying Vega would stop me and beg me not to go, but he acted as if I wasn't even in the house. "Arrogant son of a bitch." I thought to myself

I rolled my suitcases on to the car and placed them in the backseat, watching the front door to see if he would open it, I sat in the car 45 min and then I went back inside. Vega still in the same spot in front of the TV neither of us said a word as I snuggled up next to him on the sofa. placing my head on his chest. In my heart I knew I really didn't want to leave him. I was never gonna leave him. With him is where I belong.

$$$$$$$$$$$$$$$$$$$$$$$$$$$$$

Capone texted my phone early the next morning (Can u get away) his company was just what I needed. I could always vent to him about the shit that was going on between me a Vega. I replied (Give me an hour)

He told me to meet him downtown by the water. It was one of our meeting spots. Don't know why we felt anywhere in Memphis was safe

"SHYNE"

for us to meet, Vega held the keys to the city. Literally.

The wind coming off the water always made the air cold. I watched as he got off his bike. I hated bikes I always thought they were dangerous. But he made it look damn good.

"You wanna ride with me?" He kissed my lips and gave my back a squeeze "You know I ain't getting on no bike." We walked over to a bench to watch the water he threw his jacket over my shoulders

"I love it out here." I placed my head on his chest Even though I couldn't swim I loved the water I'm a cancer water is my element. I loved to be near it and I loved the sound of the rain

"My mom use to bring me and my little sister out to this same exact spot when we were little." He said enjoying his peace with him the moment felt so right. It was as if no one else was around we were out in public like it was the right thing to do.

"I need to talk to you about something." He said

"Talk" I said

KARMA

"SHYNE"

"I think we should slow shit down stop seeing each other. We can't keep this shit up" he said

"Why?" I asked.

"You know why, this shit don't feel right." He said

"So, is that it? That's the reason you brought me out here." I threw his jacket off my shoulders

"It's not like that. You don't understand, I really care about you. I don't want you hurt, I wouldn't be able to forgive myself if something happened to you. I'm a man I can handle whatever's coming for me, but—" I interrupted him

"You know what, I don't even care. You don't want to fuck with me. No need to explain I'm a big girl remember." My pride was hurt more than anything how could he reject me; no man rejects me. I wasn't even focus on the bigger picture. If Vega found out he would kill us both. He grabs my hand as I stood to leave. I snatched it from him and walked back to my car leaving him

"SHYNE"

on the bench his hands covering his face in frustration.

$$$$$$$$$$$$$$$$$$$$$$$$$$$

It was my 20th birthday Vega was throwing me a party at club Premiere my favorite artist lil Boosie was performing it was perfect. Me and the family Vega, Capone, Twain and Princess were seated in an all-white VIP it was a little awkward me and Capone hadn't spoken in weeks, but here he was starring a hole through my ass. That's why I didn't trust men they're fucking unstable. He was the one who suddenly developed a conscious and broke it off with me. I was feeling good, so I thought I'd give his ass something to look at. I got up and danced for

Vega.

I wore a Gucci halter dress with slits up the sides and no panties, so my ass was extra loose. While most men tripped on their girl for dressing like this. Vega loved for me to dress like a whore.

I knew Capone was watching my every move as I was being extra all over Vega. I was smiling inside knowing he was watching and it wasn't a damn thing he could do about it. Serves his ass right. After my lap dance with Vega.

I walked to the restroom to do me a line in one of the stalls. I sat there for a minute getting my mind together before I went back out. I walked to the sink to make sure my appearance was together. I must've been too high I saw Capone come in the bathroom and lock the door. No, this shit was really happening this nigga done lost his mind Vega is right outside. It must've been the coke I was turned on like a light. The thought of his hands on my body sent chills through my veins. He grabs me by my neck kissing me aggressively his hand underneath my dress. I wanted him to fuck me so bad I could hardly stand it.

"This what you want?" he whispered

YES!!YES!!YES! I wanted to scream he bent me over the sink no need to raise my dress my ass was already out. As he slid his thickness in me

"This what you like." I couldn't say a word he was handling me so ruff I guess this was his way of thanking me for the little dance I gave

"SHYNE"

Vega. I didn't care I was loving that shit. I threw my ass back, he grip my ass even tighter as he moved in and out, he sped up his pace. I sped up mine gripping his dick with each stroke. I'm a beast at this shit and its time he knew it. He was fucking me so good I didn't want it to end we both damn near passed out from the orgasm. Trying hard to catch our breath the loud music quickly bringing me back. Capone didn't say a word as he zip his pants and walked out the door. I grab some wet napkins I keep in my purse wiping his scent from my body getting myself together before I went back and joined the party. Vega probably thought I was high and stuck in the bathroom which I did often so he wasn't suspicious if I took a while to return.

I took my seat beside Princess "What were you doing in there?" she asked I looked at her sideways "bitch you all in my business." I thought to myself she must've read it

"You had the door locked that's why I asked." "You checking on me?" I snapped Vega

"SHYNE"

better get his nosey ass Pitbull "No, I needed to use the restroom," she answered Yeah right

"Well, if you must know I don't like people walking in on me while I'm snorting cocaine." I was all in her face. She rolled her eyes

One of Vega's friends came to join us in VIP a tall cute light skin guy. Vega introduced him to everybody. "This my man Ace, Ace this my girl." Vega said

"Nice to meet you." I said shaking his hand. I don't know what he said back but, all I heard was

"Shut the fuck up bitch" I recognize that voice anywhere. I snatched my hand back. He must've read my thoughts he looked nervous as he took his seat beside Vega never taking his eyes off me. I knew I had to make a decision. If I made the wrong decision, he might get alarmed I saw princess scrolling through her phone and I got an idea. I sent princess a message (Ace is the dude who tried to rob me.) she was being really cool not even looking up from her message as Ace snake ass smiled really good in Vegas face. Princess placed her phone back in her jacket

KARMA

pocket and pulled out a silencer sending 3 piercing bullets threw his heart.

"WHAT THE FUCK PRINCESS?" Vega screamed jumping up from the table "He's a snake we gotta go right now boss." She placed the gun back in her jacket as if nothing happened. Everybody looking at princess like she had lost her mind. Capone and twain instantly took their guns out

"You ok ma?" Vega asked me I shook my head yes

"Come on let's go" he grab my arm

"Princess get the car." He then turned towards me

"I need you to go with Twain and Capone they gonna keep you safe" But I wanted to be with him I had no idea what was going on. I was scared to death

"No Vega I want to stay with you" I wined like a child

"Don't argue with me on this ma" Twain instantly grab me taking me with him and Capone as we exited the club from the side door. I could hear gunfire in the distant Capone drew his gun

"SHYNE"

and shot 3 men before we made it to the car. I had no idea where Vega was or even if he was alive. Capone sped out the parking lot Twain still shooting out the window.

"Stay down" he yelled at me as we fled the scene
Capone was driving 100 miles an hour. "It was a hit!" Twain yelled

"Yea Twain I can fucking see that." Capone frustrated

"Is Vega ok" no one answered me

"I hope so" Capone phone rang

"V what's up. Yea we ok we going to my crib." He hung up

"He good, he gonna meet us at the crib, are you ok" he asked

"I'm good" I really wasn't the shit I was going through I only saw on TV or read in books. this shit was wild

Vega and princess were there when we made it. I was so excited to see him I threw my whole body on him he squeezed me tight. "Look here ma I'm a need you to stay here for a few days." my heart almost stops

Page | 115

KARMA

"SHYNE"

"What? No, why can't I stay with you?" I pouted like a child

"Don't argue with me right now pepa, its dangerous for you to be around me right now." I didn't care I was in love with dangerous at this point.

"I don't care Vega; I'm going with you."

I saw Capone watching me act like a fool in love knowing the outcome if Vega wanted me to stay, I was staying.

"You can't right now. I promise when its safe I'll be back for you, but right now my only concern is making sure nothing happens to you." His mind was made up he kissed me on my forehead. I just stood there with a frown on my face letting him know I didn't agree.

"Take care of her homie" I heard him tell Capone as tears rolled down my face. I prayed he would return safe. Capone house was just what I expected nice and neat like a woman lived there. "You don't want to stay with me?" I could tell he was jealous, but I could give two shits. I just wanted to get the hell out of there. I was ready to go home. I was done with this life. I headed for the door I was really having a mental breakdown. He jumped in my way.

"Come on girl, don't do this right now." He wouldn't move out of my way "Ain't no ride out there how you gonna leave." He was right Twain was gone home in his truck

"I'll walk" I said,

"Will you calm down for one second." He tried pleading with me

"NO" I tried to reach around him twisting the doorknob. He bear hugged me throwing me on the sofa.

"It's not safe. I don't even know what's going on myself. Stay till daylight then if you still want to leave, I'll take you myself." Me thinking he was telling the truth relaxed a little.

"I'm gonna let you up. You not gonna run off, is you?" he asked. I shook my head no. then he let me up as he answered his phone that's been ringing for the past 20 min.

"What up" he answered removing his shirt to reveal his sleeve of tattoos "I'm busy right now I'm a have to hit you back later" he was walking around the house making himself comfortable

"SHYNE"

"Nawl, I ain't with no bitch." I could hear him talking to who I guessed was his latenight date. I couldn't believe I was a little jealous. He ended his call and came back to me. Capone was a different kind of bad boy, not like Vega. If you saw him on any regular day, he looked nothing like a killer maybe a thug but definitely no killer but looks could never be trusted. I think that's what kept me drawn to him.

"How many?" I asked him

"How many what?" he said confused

"People have you killed." He looked confused

"None" he answered quickly

"Come on I saw you kill 3 niggas tonight" I said, "Correction you saw me shoot 3 niggas" he said "Whatever, then how many people have you shot?" I asked

"I don't know I don't keep count" he said "You lying, I know that shit has to fuck with you, haunt your dreams and shit" I waited for his response "You don't have to be tough with me I'm not that nigga" I teased him with his owns words.

"SHYNE"

"Fo'real shorty I don't know, what made you ask me that. Who ask people them kind of questions. You tripping." Seeing he didn't want to have this conversation I changed the subject "Never mind I need some clothes to put on"

I was ready to shower, go to bed. "what yo think I'm a cross dresser." He joked. "No stupid, but I can't wear this all weekend ain't no telling when Vega will be back." I pointed to my short dress

"I'll find you something." He went to his room and came back with a white tee and jogging shorts "This the best I can do." He smiled "It's perfect" I went to take a shower rummaging through his cabinets to see if I could find traces of a women, but I didn't. I went to join him in the living room watching TV.

"So, what's up what we gonna do until this is all over." He asked. I threw my legs across his

"I don't know, first you say you don't want to fuck with me then you bend me over the bathroom sink" I said

"SHYNE"

He chuckled "That shit was wild. I don't know what you do to me. I saw you tonight and I couldn't help myself. I'm in love." He rub his hands up and down my thighs. I must've been hearing things. Did this nigga just say he loved me

"What we gonna do about it" I asked confused "I just know tonight; I didn't give a fuck who knew who found out." He said seriously. Now I knew he had lost it. Vega would kill us both. He kissed my lips
"I can't live without you." He said This is what I was talking about, Capone was so different, so sweet, I was trapped. What was I gonna do? This time I wrote a check my ass couldn't cash
$$$$$$$$$$$$$$$$$$$$$$$$$$$$$$$$
After about 5 days Vega was back, which meant whoever put the hit out on him was dead. I hated to leave Capone we really connected but there was no future for us. Without one of us ending up dead. I could tell he hated to watch me leave I blew him a kiss goodbye before getting in the car with Vega.

"SHYNE"

"I miss you ma." Vega looked at me "I miss you more." I held his hand as he drove us home

"Gotta surprise for you" he said.

"What is it?" I asked knowing it would be something good anytime he went away and came back he always brought me expensive gifts.

"You'll see" he smiled when we pulled up to the house there was a white Aston martin parked in my spot.

"Ain't no way" my mouth was wide open Vega smiled at me as I jumped out looking all around the car, I couldn't wait to drive this back home no one had one of these.

Vega handed me the keys I was all grins. Vega was full of surprise's that's what I loved about him

"I love it" I said "I knew you would. Happy birthday" he told me "Let's see what she's made of" I told Vega as I got in the driver's seat starting up my new car "Where we going" he climbed in "Anywhere" I was excited as I drove around town with Vega on the passenger side, both of us behind designer sunglasses life was perfect.

$$$$$$$$$$$$$$$$$$$$$$$$$$$$$

"SHYNE"

I sat on the toilet seat holding the pregnancy test in my hands I didn't know why I was taking it in the first place I knew in my heart it was positive. "FUCK" I threw the test against the wall and cried like a baby. "My luck" this shit was unreal how could I be so fucking careless and stupid.

I paced the floor trying to think my brain seems to be cloudy. I rushed downstairs to find the phone book to call the abortion clinic I made an appointment for the following week. I didn't even believe in abortions as long as the shoe was on the other feet. I wrapped the test and the box in some paper towels and stuffed it in my purse. I planned on throwing it out on the highway to keep Vega from finding it. I wanted to get high, funny thing was I didn't want to harm the baby I was plan on killing anyway. Feeling sick between my thoughts I started throwing up. What the hell, there was no way I was having this baby.

I don't got time for this shit this was a matter of life and death to get rid of my unborn child, but who's life would it be. I had to get out of there. I needed some fresh air. Vega was out getting ready for his annual bike show tomorrow. I

texted Capone (Can I see you) he replied (At the crib)

He was in deep conversation when I arrived, but he still greeted me with a big bear hug as usual. Must've been a woman on the other end the way he was grinning. How fucking rude nigga, you was just in love with me or at least that's what you said. I can't believe I was jealous what should I expect from him. It wasn't like he could be with me. I was being selfish but I didn't give a damn, must've been the pregnancy hormones. I reached in my bag and placed the test in his face, just to be mean of course. I wasn't even thinking about what I was doing. I wanted his ass off that phone and paying me some damn

attention. I got my wish

"Ima call you back." He didn't even give her time to respond,

"You serious, this yours?" he pointed to the test "No, I just ride around with other women's pregnancy test in my bag." I said with an attitude He blew hot air out his lungs in frustration sat down and rub his temples

"Is it mine?" he asked Now I'm frustrated, really nigga "I don't know" I said honesty

"You gonna keep it." I couldn't believe we were having this conversation I never had plans to tell him or Vega

"No" I shook my head

"Then why fucking tell me" he looked disappointed "I don't know I didn't come over to tell you honestly. I just needed to clear my thoughts." I plead "I don't know what to do." I wanted to cry "You love stressing a motherfucker out I see." Capone

I felt bad for opening my mouth "I'm sorry." I got up to leave he grab me by my hand "No, I'm sorry you know I got your back whatever decision you make." He placed his hands on my stomach

"So, you really want to get rid of her." he said looking down at my stomach "How do you know it's a girl?" he placed his head on top of mine

"A father knows."

"SHYNE"

$$$$$$$$$$$$$$$$$$$$$$$$$$$$$$$$$$

It was a beautiful day; it wasn't too hot just the right amount of wind was blowing. As expected, the bike show was all that and more. Vega's boys from Texas came down even a couple of celebs were there. Trae the truth, David banner and lil flip. This was the biggest bike show of the year. Dub magazine was there the show was being recorded for TV, fly ass car's and bikes were everywhere. Half-naked women looking for the next baller.

I was seated in my Aston martin lawn seat that came with my car dressed in an all-white Versace jumper. Vega had tricked my car out, so I was mean on the scene also. I looked really good behind my Versace sunglasses; my deep wave weave pass reached my ass.

Capone was getting ready for his race, his bike was the fastest, there was no way anyone was beating him today. Vega had just picked his bike up from his boy Magic. He was the best in the game when it came to speed. Me and Capone hardly spoke a word to each other that day.

"SHYNE"

Everything we said we said with our eyes.
"Get ready Capone up next." Vega yelled to the
camera crew

Vega made big money selling these CDs.
Capone name on anything boost the sells he was
the Peyton Manning of the bike world. The crowd
went wild as he hit the start line. I looked around
at the crowd screaming his name, I couldn't help
but to be happy for him. I smiled as he sped
down the track doing what seem like 200 mph.
the sound of the bike still ringing in my ear, as I
watched it hydro plane off the tracks an into the
air. Capone's body going in a different direction.
The sound of the crash heard around the world,
made my ear's go deaf. I couldn't hear anything
the world went silent everything and everybody
around me were moving so fast towards the
scene. Vega running to the track screaming and
shouting. I moved in slow motion. God, please let
him be ok I'm sorry I wanted to kill the baby
please God let him be ok. I'll have the baby if you
just let him be ok. I tried bargaining with God. I
slowly kept moving towards the scene. I saw Vega
holding his head with tears in his eyes. Twain was

holding his head a shouting also I knew it couldn't be good. Vega saw me and started pointing telling me to get back, but not before I saw Capone's body lying motionless on the ground. His feet pointed towards the sky. His torso facedown. I let out a horrifying scream. Princess quickly grab me forcing me back away from the crowd. Tear's running down my face as she tried to calm me, but there was no calming me as my body went limp. The image of his body burning a hole in my mind. Princess helped me to the car. I sat there crying my heart out. He was gone Capone was dead.

$$\$$$

There were no words to describe the atmosphere in our home that night. "I know he was like family to you too." Vega said emotional. I didn't say a word "You gonna be ok here by yourself, I need to go talk with Capone's mother about the funeral arrangement?" Vega asked me

my heart went out to his mother, she now has no living children. I shook my head yes still not

"SHYNE"

opening my mouth. Even though I hated being in the big house by myself. I wanted to be alone, I kept seeing his body wishing it was all dream tears rolled down my cheeks. I closed my eyes to get rid of the images, I couldn't trust my thoughts. I just wanted the pain to end. Maybe when I awake, I would see his face again. I cried myself to sleep. I don't know what time I woke up to guns in my face.

"Don't fucking move, where's Vega?" the tall man in all black asked me, but this time it wasn't stick up kids it was law enforcement.

"I don't know." I threw my hands up half asleep. He grab me forcefully by my arm out of the bed an onto the floor.

"I'm pregnant" I shouted hoping he would let me go, "Cuff her ass." He threw me to the female officer, there were 13 other men with guns standing in our bedroom. The guy throwing me around was the ranking officer I'm assuming he was the one giving all the orders. For some reason he looked really familiar. I know this white man, but I don't know from where. That shit was gonna bother me all day.

"SHYNE"

"Did she tell you where he was?" I heard one of

the men ask the ranking officer. He shook his

head no.

"Where is he that's a good fucking question?" I thought to myself as the female took me to the sofa while her coworkers tore up our shit. I could hear loud walkie talkies all over the house I knew this shit was real.

"Ma'am we need you to tell us where Vincent hides his drugs, we have information that they are here in this house, this is your only chance. I repeat your only chance to save yourself. Once I leave this room and find the dope and I will find it. All deals are off the table. Do you understand me." The familiar white cop said.   "Tell us where the fuck Vincent at." The female officer yelled calling out Vega's government name

I had no idea where he was, I was hoping he showed up to save me like always, but this time I had run out of lives. I kept my cool

KARMA

"SHYNE"

"Am I under arrest." I said cocky I definitely been watching too much law an order I was scared to death. My dumbass should've been trying to be on my best behavior since I really didn't know shit and Vega had left me for dead.

"No" she said with an attitude "Then fuck you." I rolled my eyes an sat back on the couch like a real thug prepared to go to jail only difference was, I was no thug, and last time in jail I almost died.
"Ok bitch suit yourself." she walked off

I watched as they continued to terrorize the house "Where is he?" I said to myself this shit was not happening I wanted to cry but not in front of them. They were cutting up the furniture breaking glass just being rude for no damn reason. I heard a loud boom like a bomb went off I don't know what the hell they were doing. Then one of them whistled to the lieutenant. I turned around to see they had dug a hole through the kitchen floor.

"Is that it." Lieutenant asked smiling big "We about to find out." He took the machine an

"SHYNE"

opened up the floor some more "Stop stop stop."
Lieutenant waving his hands the machine
cut off "BINGO" he said
I was on the edge of my seat not even I knew
what was in there. I'm pretty sure I didn't want
to know either. All I could think about was where
the hell was Vega? "You wanna talk now smart
ass." The female cop held up a kilo of heroin

"SHYNE"

EULOGY

I held my 6lb 5oz baby girl in my arms she was so beautiful much much more then I. Her hand curled around my finger as I pressed her face next to mine. The smell of her innocence I would forever hold on too. I searched her eyes to see if I could identify her father. She could be Capones she could be Vega's. I didn't care all I knew is she was mine.

"10 more minute." The correctional officer yelled through the door, rushing me to hand off my daughter to my aunt. As you can see, I never made it to the abortion clinic. I guess she was meant to be here. I kissed her lips smelling her neck before I handed her to my aunt. She let out a small wine almost drove me insane not to be able to comfort her, as my aunt quickly rocked her back to sleep

"SHYNE"

"She's beautiful looks just like you did when you were born." My aunt smiled at her she never could have any children. Who would've thought that would be my purpose in life, to have her a child she could raise as her own? I knew she would give her the love she need. Vega never did come to my rescue, the cops found 40 kilos hidden throughout the house. I turned over my inheritance to my aunt. My mother didn't even bother to show up at the birth of her grandchild. "I gotta go sweetheart" my aunt held my sweet baby girl over for me to kiss her one last time. I took in all her beauty as I looked into her eyes. The next time I'd see my precious baby girl she would be 15 or 25 years old.

"SHYNE"

Vega's Truth

Some of you think I'm a coward for letting my girl take the fall but fuck how they think. They had played me from the very beginning, assuming I didn't know what was going on. Come on who the fuck I look like. My boy of all people. I had mad love for dude, how could he. I feed this nigga and he turned me over to the Feds for some pussy, good thing Ken was on my payroll. Pepa might've recognized him from the racetrack the first time I took her. Maybe, maybe not she stayed too fuck'd up. Capone had to go; the nigga was a Deadman the first time the thought came across his mind to fuck over me. His bike was no accident I had my man Magic to fuck with his breaks so they would only work from the starting point, he was never leaving that track alive. He was the only one who knew where my stash was hell pepa didn't even know. I really did love her I thought about taking her with me that night because I knew they were coming, but she was all sad, crying and shit over a nigga she had been fucking right under my noise. I should've killed the

"SHYNE"

bitch as well, but I'll let her suffer for the disrespect, can't turn a hoe into a housewife. That was my mistake plus someone had to take the fall. As for my daughter daddy will be to get you soon.

"SHYNE"

ENERGY

"SHYNE"

Book II Energy

48 months, 6 days, 9 hours, and 13 minutes Energy was now a free man. Not that he was a stranger to doing time. He been in and out the system since he was 15. He started selling drugs at the age of 10. Like most drug dealers, he learned nothing from prison, but how to be a smarter criminal. Only problem was this time around, he was dead broke. He'd lost everything when he went in. He spent his money on lawyers, legal fees, and his sisters college education. He needed money, and he needed it fast. This time he had it all figured out, a solid proof plan to never be broke again.

His sister Reagan waited for him outside the tall barb wire fence.

"AAAAAAhhhhhhh," she started screaming running up to hug him. She missed her brother so much. He spoiled her rotten. Their mother was doing life in prison for the murder of their father and his live-in girlfriend. They were raised by their uncle, their fathers baby brother, who did the best he could when he wasn't drinking. That's mainly the reason Energy started selling drugs, to support them.

Energy born Quadarius Miller. Was 28 years old with dark skin smooth like butter, slanted eyes, and full lips. He had a large muscular frame from the daily workouts. Prison had preserved his youth, so he didn't look a day over 20. Reagan was beautiful also; she looked a lot like her brother, only she had her mother's light skin.

"Damn girl, you done grew up on me." He examined his 21-year-old sister. It's been 14 months since he last saw her. He had been placed in a prison 10 hours from home and he didn't want her driving to visit him. That's how federal prison works, you could be clear across country and it wasn't a damn thing you could do about it.

"Me, look at you" She grabs his big bicep. "You know I been getting my sexy on." He smiled. "I hope this the last time I gotta pick yo sexy ass up from this hell hole." She said.

"Oh, it will be, trust me" They walked to her BMW. "Damn you still got this car." He had bought it for her for high school graduation.

"SHYNE"

"Yes, I do" She said with attitude. "We gotta get you a new whip, ain't no way you drove this car all way out here. It bet not break down on us." He laughed

"I don't know what you talking about, ain't nothing wrong with my beamer," she pulled off the lot leaving the prison in their rearview.

"I hope you finna take a nigga to eat. I'm hungry as hell," He rubbed his stomach. "I passed this nice seafood place on the way in. We could stop there; I know you missing them shrimps you loved." She said,

"Baby sister can afford shrimps, look at you." He smiled

"I just got my school check; money Is no problem. Plus, I been saving a little money for when you come home. It's not the money you use too, but it's a start." She said,

"Ok baller, let a broke nigga hold something." He joked "First we need to find a mall and get you out of those whack ass shoes and whatever that is you wearing." They both laughed.

KARMA

"SHYNE"

"How shit been out here?" He asked looking out the window at freedom. He dreamed about this day for a long time.

"Same ole same ole, ain't shit really changed. You act as if you been locked up a quarter century." She joked.

"Feel like it hell. What happened to Easy?" He asked about his childhood friend.

"Wanted to be a damn stick-up kid and got his ass fucked up." She spat

"I hate that shit, niggas was eating when I was out here, especially Easy, he would've never had to rob a motherfucker if I—" she interrupted. "Don't blame yourself for his fuck up. You live by the sword; you die by the sword." He said. Easy was murdered a year after Energy got locked up. Energy blamed himself for Easy's death because he depended on him.

"What you know about a sword?' he laughed. "I ain't as corny as you think, I am from the hood you know." She said,

"No nigga, I'm from the hood, yo ass from Beverly Hills." He was right, Energy lived the hood life but by the time Reagan started high school, he bought a house in the suburbs.

"I guess it's just in me then." She chuckled. "We will make it home tomorrow. I booked us a room in Texas for tonight." She wasn't driving all night to Mississippi.

"That's cool, how's Monique?" He asked, Reagan rolled her eyes, but knew the question was coming. Monique was Reagan best friend since the sandbox. They were thicker than thieves. Monique spent many nights at Reagan's house when they were younger. That's how she developed a relationship with Energy. She was 14 the first time they had sex. He was 17. She always had a crush on him, and him being young, he jumped on the opportunity to do a virgin. She feel headfirst in love, but Energy was young. He could've cared less for Monique. She was not attractive, brown skin 4 ft
10 inches, and shape funny. He would never acknowledge her in the light of day. She was just easy pussy to a 17-year-old boy at the time.

Reagan remained neutral between their relationship, or at least she tried. Monique was her only friend in grade school. When their mother first went to prison, they struggled, barley having enough to eat and not even descent clothes to wear.

Monique would meet Reagan in the restroom before first period with a name brand change of clothes, so the other kids would stop picking on her. She even gave Reagan brand-new sneakers off her feet and told her parents someone stole them in P.E. Monique's parents were both doctors from the hood but didn't want their daughter growing up spoiled, so they left her in public school. She still got whatever she wanted. Reagan would be forever loyal to her as a friend.

"At home I guess, you should know." She sassed. "She was good to me over these last past years, hell she was more than good. She made sure I had it." He bragged

"Yeah, I know." Reagan hated the way Monique was a fool for Energy. He treated her like shit and she loved the ground he spit on. All he wanted was what she had to offer him.

"SHYNE"

"I need that to be our first stop tomorrow." He said

"Why, so you can continue to mind, fuck her."

He couldn't believe Reagan was in her feelings. She never commented on his business. He knew Reagan loved Monique, but he was her first love.

"Mind fucking, how you sound?" He couldn't hide his smile.

"Yeah, like you been doing all her life. I can't believe she's so gullible, no let me rephrase that, so damn dumb." She was getting heated thinking about it.

"I ain't mind-fucking nobody." He "What you call it, you know damn well you don't give a fuck about her. You gonna get her money, her car, and then stay gone for days. She'll be calling me crying, then you will come back and do it all over again." She said,

"It's not my fault, she's caught up in a fantasy, Reagan." He defended himself

"A fantasy you've been selling her since she was 13." She said

"SHYNE"

"14," he corrected her.

"Whatever" she rolled her eyes.

"You know that girl has never been with nobody else. She want even give herself a chance to be happy, just wasting time on your dog-ass." She spat

"Ouch sis," he grabs his chest still unbothered.

Reagan was right, Monique was so in love, thinking he would one day love her the way she loved him. She never had time to find real love. At 16 She had even been pregnant by him. She was so happy thinking he would love her. After all she was carrying his firstborn. When she told him, he flipped out on her and gave her 500 to have an abortion, Monique was devastated. He started feeding her lines about her future and how she needed to attend college. She was going to do whatever made him happy. Reagan drove her heart broken friend to the abortion clinic. It was one of the worst days of Reagan's life. She felt terrible for her friend.

"I'm just saying, I'm a female, would you like if a nigga dogged me?" she said. He couldn't even contemplate the thought of someone hurting Reagan, especially the way he hurt women.

"I'll kill a mother fucker about you and you know that." He said,

"Don't say that" Reagan didn't like when he talked about killing, she knew he was serious, "And end back up in there?" She snap.

"You all I care about, and if a mother fucker fuck with you, you the only reason I'll go back." She didn't respond.

 She knew she was wasting her breath. Her words were going in one ear and out the other.

"I just don't want to be in the middle of your shit. Karma is real! One day we all have to pay for our shit. Monique my girl, like the sister I never had."

Energy chuckled. "So, you wanted a sister?" He said not taking her serious.

"Don't worry about it" she was annoyed.

"I feel you sis, it's just the way us men are. I've tried to be with just one woman but I can't," he said.

"SHYNE"

"You gonna end up with something you can't get rid of, nasty butt." She spat.

"Girl I just left the Pen. They check yo ass for everything. EVERYTHING, I'm cleaner than the State Board of Health." He bragged. She couldn't help but smile at her foolish brother. She missed his company for many years. She felt safe with him around. She took him shopping. They spent the night in Texas and was headed to Monique house wide open.

Energy was the man before he left the streets. They loved and feared him at the same time. He took good care of Reagan, unlike in grade school. In high school, she had the best of everything, which made her popular really quick. She wore nothing but the best and got drop off in limo's for every event. Energy had her spoiled. Everyone wanted to be close to her, but she only fucked with Monique. She was with her while she was starving, so that's who she chose to eat with. Real recognize real.

Monique had been impatiently waiting for them to arrive. She kept money on his books and accepted every call from prison. She was his

"SHYNE"

Bonnie or at least she wanted to be. In prison she had been his one true love. She was supposed to pick him up, but close to his release date, he fed her a story about Raegan wanting to spend time with him. She believed it because she knew how close they were, and basically all the family they had were each other. Even if she didn't, she wouldn't ask Raegan if it was true. She would never put her in that situation. Energy was her family. She knew who she would choose, but none of that matter's right now, Energy was home.

She smiled so big when she saw him, throwing her arms around his strong body!

"Hey baby" Monique said. "

What's up girl" He hugged her tight, landing a kiss on her forehead.

"I'm gonna be sick," Raegan teased walking into the house. She couldn't stand the fakeness.

"What you got to eat in here?" she open the fridge.

"My baby home, we going out to eat," Monique smiling from ear to ear. She was ready to spoil him.

"SHYNE"

" Let me jump in the shower" Energy said.
"Go head bae" she pointed him in that direction.
It was her and Energy against the world.
Monique wasn't any ordinary women; she was
about her paper. She owned her home and 3
luxury cars. She graduated top of her class and
was now in her First year of the medical field.
He walked into the master bedroom and saw all
the shoes and clothes all over the room. Brand
new and nothing but the best, all for him. "I
could get use to this" he wasn't surprised. He
knew she would go over and beyond not to be
out done.

"You like" she watched him grab the
newest Air Jordan out the box. "Hell, yeah bae,
you did good" he said.

Monique eyed him with lust. She couldn't
wait to get him in her bed. Energy was the sexiest
man alive in her eyes, and 4yrs in a Federal
Penitentiary, he couldn't wait to knock the
headboard out of her California king size bed.
Monique might've not been the sexiest women
alive to him, but they always had the best sex. He
had trained her from a young age, and no matter

how many women he slept with, nobody could give head like she could. His dick jumping at the thought.

She jumped on him knocking them both down on the bed.

"Damn bae can a nigga bathe first?" he asked,

"Your dick doesn't think so." she could fill his man hood at full salute. She unbutton his pants, kissing all over him.

"Where's Rae?" he ask.

She's gone," she said in between breath's. He placed his hands on the small of her back.

"Take a shower with me" he said looking her in her eyes. Monique was hypnotize. "Whatever you want," she pecked his lips quickly removing her clothes. He seen her body numerous times but wished the room was dark. His dick already on hard, at that point it didn't matter what her body looked like. They made love in the shower, then in the bedroom.

Monique was out cold just as Energy planned. He took another shower, drowned himself in the unforgettable cologne she had

"SHYNE"

bought him. He got dressed and hit the brick's in her all-white Lexus, sunroof open, music blazing through the 15's. He went to the hood to visit his man Bone. He saw Aunt T sitting on the porch of the run-down house. The grass hadn't grown in years from all the car's parked on it. He thought about his sister's word's, shit really don't change. Bone stepped out on the porch looking confused, until he notice who was behind the wheel.

"I know that ain't my boy." Bone was a nice looking tall light skin man. He had gold teeth top and bottom, wide eyed, and a dimple in his left check. He wore a low afro and a goatee.

"Glad you at the crib, my nigga" he grabbed Energy's hand pulling him in for a hard embrace. People are glad to see you, even though they ain't sent you shit while you were locked up, and after you finish doing time none of that even matter's to you anymore. They be the first people you go see. Energy didn't care one way or the another, he was a man. He didn't expect shit from a nigga. He held his own.

"Who ride" Bone asked.

"SHYNE"

"Monique." He said,

"Monique doing it big I see," eyeing the Lexus. Bone was one of the few people who knew about their relationship. "So, where we headed?" he jump in the car.

"To the moon nigga, where you think?" Energy said.

"I'm game" They went out to a local night club called Black Street. It's the spot where everyone hangs out at, until a fight breaks out or shots get fired. It's been closed several time's and reopen under new management. If It was one thing, Bone was good for; it was finding women and a good party. The streets were packed with long lines of car's waiting to park.
It had been a long time for Energy, but this was what he was used to. These were his streets.

"Look at the hoe's out here," he smiled at Energy. Who remained cool. He really didn't have his ass on a woman, they flocked to him most of the time. He wanted to get a feel of the environment he was about to step back into, to see who was doing what.

KARMA

"SHYNE"

Most drug dealers like to spend big money on VIP, and bottle service, so he was at the perfect place.

"We bout to find you some pussy." He told him. " A- Yo" he hollered at the group of women walking towards the door. Bone was hanging halfway out the window as the women approach the car. They were twisting their hips with all there might as they walked to the Lexus.

"How y'all ladies doing tonight?" Bone asked the group of women. Energy still played the background, thinking about how wild Bone was. He was still the same nigga, A womanizer.

"We bout to go in the club, what's up with y'all?" the dark skin girl said.

"We bout to do the same. I want y'all to meet my man Energy, he just making it home." He introduced him

"Energy, what's up," the light skin girl excited to see him. He looked confused.

"Do I know you?" he asked,

"That's Summer, you remember Jeremy?" Bone lean in to tell him. Energy shook his head in agreement recognizing the now grown-up little girl.

"That's his little sister" bone whispered. "Word," he couldn't believe how sexy she was. She was only 19 but looked 25. "Word," Bone smiled showing all golds. He knew Energy approved.

"What's good little momma?" He felt the need to get better acquainted.

"You, I'm glad you finally home?" she said smiling in his face, everyone knew who he was and like any gold digger. She was thinking, I'll get to him before the next bitch, so she was making a lasting impression.

"Finally," he agreed.

"My nigga back in position." Bone said proudly. Even though he didn't keep in touch while Energy was in prison, he knew he would be back on the throne soon. He would make it up to him by kissing his ass now that he was home. Bone was playing his cards to make sure he got the #2 crown.

"SHYNE"

"What you getting into later?" she lean in the car so he could get a better look at her breast, they were screaming for a looser top.

"Hoping to see you." He answered. "Take my number." He pulled out the cell phone Monique had given him and saved her number. "I'll call you." he said

"I'll be waiting" her and her friends walked off.

Soon as Energy stepped through the doors. The familiar atmosphere filled his body. He was home and he now knew it. He loved the night life. He loved the fame of the streets. The fact that everyone knew him and most of all, feared him. BLo was the first to spot him.

"What up booooy." He ran over hugging him. "A, A this my nigga right here," he introduced him to his crew. Even Energy was shocked. Him and B-Lo were not boys, they weren't enemies but definitely not friends. They didn't care for each other. They've had a few disagreements so they mainly stayed out each other's way. Bone was short light skin with a big ass head.

"SHYNE"

"It's good to see ya. Got something for ya too boy believe that." He bragged. "Hold this" he told his boy handing him the bottle of Moet. He reached in the pockets of his baggy jeans and pulled out a stack of cash handing it to Energy. Which is not an uncommon greeting for a person fresh out of prison.

 "It's plenty mo where that come from." B-Lo bragged, taking a pull from his Newport. Energy knew he was a big boaster, a clown in his eyes.

"I'm good fam, appreciate it though" Energy didn't want a handout from him. He knew he would want something in return.

"Ok cool." He placed his money back in his pants. "Send 2 more bottle's up to my VIP," B-Lo told the waiter as he escorted Energy in the direction like they were BFF. Energy laughed in the inside. He wasn't a fool; he was everybody's nigga now that he was a free man. He might as well enjoy tonight if B-Lo wanted to trick off his money on bottle service all night, then who was he to stop him. People were in and out of VIP visiting him like he was the president. B-Lo wore

"SHYNE"

a fake smile but his heart was full of jealousy. He must've forgot once a king always a king.

Energy watched as Armina took a seat beside B-Lo, not even making eye contact with him. She couldn't, she had only written him 1 letter days after he went in. After that, she moved on to the next baller. Armina was supposed to be his ride or die chic, he had strong feeling for her. They were in love for many years. Seeing her next to B-Lo, he hated himself for ever loving her. Armina was what you would call a brickhouse, 36 24 36, beautiful chocolate skin, it wasn't hard for her to stop traffic at all.

"So now that you home what you trying to do? Get paid right?" B-Lo answered his own question. Blowing a line of cocaine as if there was no one else in VIP. The fact that he was a powder head twitch Energy nerves even more. "She can't be in love with this crackhead?" he thought to himself.

"We'll see" Energy wasn't fucking with him on that level. He didn't trust him for one. Plus, he had his own plug. A dude from Alabama, he met in the Fed's called Ra-Ra. "You right, take your time, whatever you need, I'm a make that shit happen." He bragged. Energy wasn't paying him any attention; his eyes were glued on Armina.

   "Sho you right" Bone spoke up.   He bought dope from B-Lo, but now that Energy was home, he knew B-Lo was about to be dethroned. B-Lo knew also that's why he would keep him close, but Energy couldn't be controlled and with him unleashed, B-Lo could be headed for early retirement.

   "You know Mina, my baby moms, right?" BLo noticed the look he had gave her earlier and felt the need to address it. He introduced her knowing Energy knew who she was. He twisted his jaw before answering.

   "Yea I do. What's up" he spoke to Armina. She just looked away not wanting to disrespect B-Lo or having to argue with him when they got home. Energy smiled; he felt the shot right through his heart. He wanted to smash B-Lo but remained cool, that was his woman she meant nothing to him anymore.

"SHYNE"

"Let's get this party crunk" Bone yelled out to the DJ; the DJ started giving them shot outs in VIP. Energy really was having the time of his life.

Bone girl Shawana join them in VIP with two of her friends.

"Yo, this my man Energy, that's Tia, Memorie and you know Shawana." He introduce them to each other.

"Nice to meet you" Tia.

"Pleasures mine" he showed a special interest in Tia. She was bowlegged which he found extremely sexy. She had a petite frame, coco skin, wide eyes, juicy lips like Kerry Washington and high cheek bones. Tia thought he was sexy also. She made it her business to sit beside him. He moved in closer to her.

"You may not want to move so close to me shorty, niggas seemed to be intimidated by me, we wouldn't want your man to get the wrong idea." He lean in to tell her. Tia smiled. She loved the way he licked his lips before he spoke.

"First of all, you moved closed to me and if that's your way of asking me if I have a man, no I don't." she said

"SHYNE"

"Ain't no way they left you amongst the single." He said,

"You must be trying to be my man?" she asked,

"Not really, just want to get to know you." he said.

"Ok I can handle that. I hear you just come home how long you been gone?" she asked.

"4 long years," he said,

"That explains why I don't know you." She said,

"What you mean everybody knows me." he said. She smiled; she loved his cockiness.

"Well, I don't" she sip her drink.

"Where you from?" he asked.

"Horn Lake, I moved here two years ago." She said.

"For what? Ain't shit around here but trouble, you a troublemaker?" he asked,

"I needed a change," she said,

"From what?" he asked,

"From life, I was missing something or someone, nosey" She laughed

"SHYNE"

"I've been in the Pen, I need to know who's around me, who I'm dealing with at all times." He said. He didn't know if he had been gone to long, but Tia was the most beautiful women he ever laid eyes on

"So, I'm around you, how come you can't be around me?" she asked

"Same thing. If you let me, I may be able to give you that change you been searching for." he said,

"You think so." she said,

"Try me." he said,

"You something serious." she told him

"I know," they shared a laugh. He loses focus of the conversation when he spots Reagan walk in with some gold teeth, gold chain wearing too much gold nigga.

"Who is that?" he patted Bone's leg. Bone looked around to see who he was talking about. "Man, that's Nino, nigga ain't shit he's harmless, stop being so overprotective, Reagan grown." Bone went back to his conversation.

"What the fuck you say" Energy who had been playing it cool all night, but the old Energy was about to show up. Everyone got paranoid, they knew he didn't play especially about Reagan. Rumor had it when he was 14, he beat the hell out of two niggas at the same damn time, not stopping to take a breath for picking on Reagan. That's when the old heads started calling him Energy. The name stuck with him. Bone wasn't a coward by far but also knew Energy played in a different league of bad boys.

"No disrespect big homie," Bone decided to mind his own business. Energy hated to see Reagan grow up, he wanted to shield her heart from niggas like him, but somethings in life he couldn't protect her from. Nino better know if he hurt's Reagan, it just might cost him his life. Energy got Tia's number before leaving the club, he dropped Bone off letting him know the business would be good soon.

He went home to his 6-bedroom empire. That he purchased for him and his family 10 years ago. He didn't even care to go upstairs to his master bedroom. He strip down to nothing but his boxers and tank top and lay on the living room sofa, in 3 minutes he was fast asleep.

"SHYNE"

$$$$$$$$$$$$$$$$$$$$$$$$$$$$$$$$$$$

"Energy," Reagan yelled trying to shake him awake. "Energy," she shook him with more force. "Yeah," he opened his eye's wiping slob from his mouth. Still slightly hungover.

"Get up and eat," she walks off to fix his plate. Reagan was always the women of the house. She cooked, cleaned, and washed whatever clothes they didn't send out to the cleaners.

Energy washed his face and brushed his teeth, thinking about how good it felt to look at himself in the mirror of his own home. His uncle was already seated at the table. It made him sad to see him now a days, he shook early mornings until he got his fix. He also had a case of dementia. Sometimes he knew where he was, other times he didn't. Only thing he knew was his Gin bottle. Either way, Energy had mad respect for him. He was the only one that kept him and Reagan from being separated when their mother first went to prison. None of the family wanted anything to do with them, since their mother killed their father as if it was their fault. They had no known relatives on their mother's side because she was a runaway from Chicago when she met their father. In Energy's eye's, his uncle was most loved and would always be his hero.

"Hey unc" Energy said. His uncle never looked up from his plate he was eating. He concentrated on finishing his food that was the only way Reagan would give him
his bottle. So, he let nothing disturb his breakfast. Energy took a seat next to him, Reagan handed him his plate then answered her ringing phone.

"You seen Energy?" Monique on the other end. Reagan gave him a look to let him know it was her. He snatch the phone damn near taking her ear off.

"What up," He said with an attitude still shoving food in his mouth.

"Where you been?" she asked.

"What?" he looked confused; she had definitely lost her mind.

"I know damn well you not questioning me, I just went through 4 years of mother fuckers telling me when and where and why." He snapped.

"SHYNE"

"I wasn't questioning you baby, I just thought I would take you out to eat today since we didn't get a chance to go last night." Reagan just shook her head, he had been out all night in Monique's car, now he was making her out to be the bad guy. If her brother was good at anything, it was reverse psychology.

Monique was just relieved he was at home and not with another women. She definitely didn't want to piss him off.

"I'll be there soon," he hit the end button. "You a mess" Reagan.

"Mind yo business," he smirked. "I told you I wasn't gonna be in the middle of your shit." She snatch her phone from him.

"I got that, who was that nigga you was with last night?" he asked,

"Who Nino." She said

"Nawl the damn Boogie man" he said sarcastically.

"What kind of a name is Nino." He joked "What kind of name is Energy." She snap back. "Don't play, who is he?"

"SHYNE"

"A friend, I am grown," placing her hand on her hip.

"I don't like him." He said

"You don't even know him" she laughed.

"And." He said

"Well, I do" she said. before Energy could snap back.

"Quadarius," his uncle recognized him. They both felt sorry for him, not wanting to upset his uncle, he let his argument go with Reagan.

"You got big boy." He said.

"I told his fat ass." Reagan smiled. "4 Years will do that to ya." He said,

"I hope you here to stay this time?" he said, "I am Unc."

His uncle got up from the table letting Reagan know he was ready for his bottle.

"I'm not done with you" Energy told Reagan before he got up from the table. She stuck out her tongue behind his back. Energy went up to his master bedroom showered and decided to air dry. He took his time getting dress, enjoying walking around his oversized bedroom. He was now comfortable again; you can't really get comfortable showering with other men.

He left his house heading nowhere near Monique's. Instead, he hit highway 78 to Alabama to holler at RA-RA, that was the name he had given his former rack mate. He called him that as a joke because he had transition to the Rastafari Religion while in the feds. He grew long dreads and even developed an accent. If you didn't know, you would think he was born Jamaican. Energy found it funny how prison changed people, Ra-Ra was released a year before him he kept in touch, even put money on his books. In prison Ra-Ra became connected to the Jamaican Mafia out of Miami. He had direct contact to Christopher Coke leader of the Shower Posse who terrorized Miami for years, known as one of the most dangerous men on the planet. Ra-Ra kept his promise to put Energy back on when he came home.

He told him he was living large but he had no idea he had a 7-car garage, and a different car for every day of the week, 18-bedroom mansion, security out the ass crawling all over the place, this was some Scarface shit fo'real.

"What's good fam" Ra-Ra embraced him.

"I told you I was coming through." Energy

"Indeed, I've been waiting." They sat up many nights in prison planning this first meeting.

"Come on in so we can talk. Trina get us a drink," he said to one of the three beautiful women in the house. One was Puerto Rican, two Jamaican Energy being a man fresh out of prison couldn't keep his eyes off of them.
"So, what are we thinking about?" Ra-Ra asked him as they sat down in the 2000 ft square front room with high maintenance furniture. Trina brought them their drinks. He gave her a polite nod then tuned into Ra-Ra. "At least 10," Energy. "No problem its done." Ra-Ra.

"I ain't got no bread yet nigga, you know I just touched down." Energy confused.

"I got you boy, don't trip." Ra-Ra

"No way I'm taking 10 keys on a front. I just needed to touch basis with you in person. Make sure we still good." He said,

"SHYNE"

"My word is my bond, I told you I got you."
Ra-Ra talking in thick accent. Energy wanted to
laugh.

"Yea but you a fake ass Jamaican wanna
be." He said to himself.

"Nigga this me you talking to speak English
motherfucker." They had that type of relationship.
Energy always teased him about his religion.

"I tell you what, bring me 20 stacks and
we'll do business. Will that ease your mind
better." Ra-Ra suggested. Energy could live with
that. He didn't like handouts. Energy staring at
Trina drifted from the conversation.

"You like her?" Ra-Ra asked.

"My bad man" Energy looked away not
wanting to be disrespectful to his friend.

"No, it's quite alright my friend. This is your
day, my gift to you." He smiled wide.

"Trina," he yelled.

"Yes" she said on que.

"Mr. Miller needs some company; can you
take care of him for me please?" he asked "Sure
boss" she slightly nodded for him to follow her.
The other two women followed command.

"SHYNE"

Energy followed the woman into the back room. Checking his pockets for his magnums. 2 hours later he was back on the highway to Mississippi. In deep thought. He had a plan to get 20 stacks and he knew exactly how he would executed it.

Monique was glad to have Energy around, he still would sneak off at night but always woke up with her. He was playing the role of the good boyfriend. She was treating him like a king. He didn't have to lift a finger. "I need your help bae," he said looking down at her laying on his chest.

"What's up" she would do anything for him at this point.

"I need some money" he said.

"It's always money" she thought.

"How much Energy" she said irritated.

"20, you don't have to if you don't want too, I promise I'll pay you back. Soon as I get straight." He promised.

Money was no object she had plenty of it. She just knew she was in a catch, 22 situation, either way he was gonna leave when she gave him what he needed but maybe this time he would know she would always have his back. She was his bonnie. Maybe this time he would see she was all he needed. Of course, she gave in. "Ok, I'll have to call the bank in the morning and sign for it, but I got you." She kissed his lips. "My girl" he praised her. Monique could've easily gotten the money. She got 200 thousand stashed in a safe deposit box. She made up the story, just so he could spend one more night because she knew by daybreak after the banks open Energy was ghost.

$$$$$$$$$$$$$$$$$$$$$$$$$$$$$$$$

"You move fast my friend." Ra-Ra was shocked to see him back so soon.

"I told you I gotta get it," he handed him the 20 thousand Monique gave him.

"I don't fuck with no broke hoes." He bragged.

"I see. Get his shit" he ordered Trina, who was smiling thinking about the sex they had. If RaRa knew she enjoyed, she might end up dead. She brought him his duffle bag with 10 bricks in it.

"I'll be back soon." He shook his hand and was on his way home. Just having the dope

"SHYNE"

around him made him feel on top of the world, the power was running through his body. His first stop was Bone, even though Bone left him for dead in prison. He knew he was about his money. He needed him; he didn't trust no one else to take care of his business. Bone always was loyal to him while he was on the street. Energy tossed the duffle bag on the kitchen table.

"What the fuck is that?" Bone asked.

"Take a guess" Energy. Bone started smiling, he knew exactly what was in the bag. His eyes glowed as he unzipped the bag.

"That's what I'm talking about,"
 "I need to move this shit dog; I owe a nigga 80 racks. I need that money first. I don't like having no nigga in my pockets," Energy looked at Bone whose eyes were still glued on the bricks.

"You listening to me dog.'' He asked,
 "Yea I heard you, 80 bands." Bone assured him.

"I'm counting on you." He said,
"You always do," he smiled.
 "Hey what's up with Mina?" Energy.

"SHYNE"

"Man, she's B-Lo girl, you know how these hoes is, out of sight out of mind." Bone.

"You got her number?" he asked. Bone looked at him sideways, he knew how Energy felt about Armina but she had moved on and he wanted no beef with B-Lo.

"Yeah, I got it, but its plenty of less stressful pussy out here. Don't be sweating her, plus B-Lo run this shit now and-" He was interrupted.

"He runs what nigga? Not me, fuck that nigga. Now is you gonna give me the number or not." Energy.

"Ok you the boss." Bone threw up his hands. Energy left his house dialing Armina's number.

"Hello" she answered.

"Can you talk?" He asked.

"Yea what's up" she recognized his voice after seeing him the other night. She knew he would be calling.

"You" he replied,

"Where you at?" he asked

"Home." She said,

"You alone?" he asked

"SHYNE"

"Yes." She said

"I'm about to swing through." He hung up.

She hurried to take a shower. She knew he must want to play. Not giving a damn about B-Lo at the time. He was on a run and wouldn't be back till the morning. She was not missing out on the opportunity to be with Energy. She knew the affect she had on him; she knew she held his heart. She put on the tightest outfit she could find. Sprayed her Victoria Secret Body perfume on her and waited.

When she saw him, she wished she could reverse time, she prayed he didn't hold any grudges against her. This day came back faster then she thought, and now all she wanted was him.

"How you been?" he asked her. "Making it," she notice his designer gear he was wearing and knew he was back, doing him. "You look good" he said.

"Thank you" she swung her hair back behind her ear's revealing her smooth chocolate skin. "Momma, momma" her son ran into the living room.

"SHYNE"

"Look I fell," he started to fake up a cry, showing his mother his bruised knee.

"Let me see" she sat him down to examine him. Energy loved watching her, she needed no makeup or nothing. Armina had a natural beauty that would drive any man crazy. Energy had been that man for years. Armina might have been the only women he ever loved besides his mother and sister, but he wasn't there for that.

"Momma who dat?," He pointed at Energy. Armina remain silent, she wanted to so badly tell him that was his father. She knew that would only confuse him. The only father he knew was B-Lo, and he would probably kill her if he found out. Armina was pregnant when Energy got locked up. She wrote him to tell him, and he never wrote back, so she did what she thought she needed to do. She slept with B-Lo and told him she was pregnant by him. B-Lo was so green to have Energy girl pregnant, he didn't give it a second thought.

"I'm Energy little man, your leg cool." He bent down to help his son. Looking deep into his eye's, any fool could see that he was Energy's, but

"SHYNE"

B-Lo was so busy wanting to be Energy, everything he saw looked like Energy.

"I'm ok now," he ran off to play. Armina didn't have any words as Energy stared at her.

"I wrote you and told you," she said her back turned to him.

"I know" he answer.

"Why you didn't. I mean what did you expect for me to do." she said,

"I didn't expect for you to tell another nigga my kid was his." Energy spat.

"You didn't you write me back." She said defensive.

"Look, I'm not here to argue, what's done is done." He said,

"Then why are you here?" she asked,

"Because I care, don't think for one second I wasn't thinking about y'all." He said.

She didn't want to trust her emotions, but she knew she still loved him.

"Where do we go from here?" She asked like a child.

"Everything gonna be alright. You trust me don't you." He tilted her chin and kissed her lips.

"SHYNE"

"I miss you" She said. "I miss you too" He squeezed her tight.

"I gotta go," Energy needed to get out of there fast. He didn't want to lose control of the situation.

This was about his son, not them.

"You leaving," she watched him walk to the door.

"I thought you came to see me?" she was disappointed,

"I came to see my son" he snap. Armina knew he could be crazy and she wasn't about to piss him off.

"You mad at me?" she asked.

"Never," he walked out the door. He had been thinking a lot about Tia. He tried to call her a couple times, but she didn't answer. Energy wasn't about to sweat no woman. Pussy was no problem, he could get it, when he couldn't eat.

"You a hard woman to connect with" he told Tia.

"Who is this?" she said

"Energy," he said

"SHYNE"

"I'm sorry, I've been missing your call's. I didn't recognize the number, and I've been working overtime. I haven't had time to do anything.

"So, what's up" she said.

"I thought you might've be dodging a nigga." He said,

"I don't play kid games, if I didn't won't to talk to you, I wouldn't have given you my number." She said.

"So, where you at?" he asked.

"Leaving work heading to the mall." She said, "Can I meet you there," he asked.

"Sure, you can." She said

She waited in the parking lot for him to pull in. "I love that car." Talking about Monique Lexus.

"Not mine, it's borrowed." He said.

"I guess you are important, people just let you borrow their Lexus." She laughed

"I guess so, what you going to buy?" He asked as she got out of her Toyota Camry, wearing her mickey mouse scrub's. She also wore Gucci frame eyeglasses. Energy loved her professional look. Tia the working girl was totally different from Tia the party girl he met the other night.

"Mother's Day gift." She said,

"I'll walk with you." he said,

"You don't got no women do you, because I don't mind smashing a bitch, if I got to." She said.

"Listen at you, you don't even look right cussing, but no. You won't have to smash a bitch." He joked

"Don't let the size fool you, dynamite come's in small packages." She smiled.

"No disrespect shorty, but fo'real I ain't got no women, I'm trying to make you my woman" he said.

She couldn't help but to smile "I thought you said, you just wanted to get to know me." she said,

"I do, so what's up." He said,

"We'll see how tonight goes." She said.

"Is that an invitation?" he ask.

"Yep" she said,

"Where you wanna go?" he asked

She thought for a few seconds.

"I haven't been bowling in a while."

"Bowling," he had never been bowling.

"SHYNE"

"Yeah, meet me there around 7:00." She said,

"Meet you where?" he asked confused

"At the bowling alley" she said

"Oh, you were serious,"

"Come on it will be fun." She said,

"Then I'm already there."

$$$$$$$$$$$$$$$$$$$$$$$$$$$$$$$$

"You mean to tell me you gave Energy ass 20 thousand dollars and you wondering why his ass is ghost. Bitch you a good one." Reagan told Monique; she had called her with usual gossip about Energy.

"You always so negative. I know how he used to be; I just thought this time." Monique

"You thought since you took care of his trifling butt in prison, he would come home and be your Prince charming, Nique this Energy come on." Reagan. "Listen to me Nique, Energy is my brother, same mother same father, no one on this earth I love more than him, but sometimes I wish you would think for you and not him." she said

"SHYNE"

"You must think I don't already know this. I got a P.H.D. bitch. I'm far from stupid, but that doesn't stop me from loving him. He bout to get his ass up out my car though." She tried to convince herself, but Reagan knew she was lying. She had no spine when it comes to Energy.

"If you say so." She said

"You think he really with someone else" Monique asked.

"Hell, yeah bitch, is you crazy? He always with someone else," Reagan wanted to say, but she'd never hurt her friends feelings like that, and wouldn't betray her brother. Monique was her friend, but Energy was her heart.

"I don't know Nique" she forced the words out. "He probably is, I'll call you back, I need to call and tell him to bring my car." Monique

"Bye" Reagan hung up frustrated.

Before his date with Tia he stops by Bone's house, Bone called earlier and told him the work was almost gone. He had to see it to believe it.

"This shit some straight drop my nigga, it ain't gone last through the night, I promise." Bone.

"SHYNE"

"All of it?" Energy was shocked before he went in. 10 keys would last him a week. The streets had changed, plus Energy had the best dope in town.

"Hell, yeah nigga, my phone jumping like the 1st and 3rd." bone.

"I guess I need to go see my man tomorrow." He counted his money and gave Bone his cut.

"Wish you could go see that nigga now, I ain't gone be able to get no damn sleep tonight." They both laughed.

"Oh yea, I meant to tell you earlier but I got busy I got a little beef. B-Lo called asking me who I was moving work for, as if he already don't know. Nigga being nosy and shit trying to see really what the fuck you got going on. Talking bout why I'm dick riding? Really nigga, the way that nigga was throwing money around in the club the other night. Man please, I told him don't call my phone again talking crazy or he gone meet Lucile." Lucile was his Glock 9.

Energy laughed, he knew niggas would have a problem with him taking the streets back, especially B-Lo, his reign as king was now over. Energy didn't care what they thought, as long as they didn't get stupid and bring any problems his way.

"Tell him he gonna have to get his paper way up to go to war with me, but I ain't never been a greedy nigga. I don't need that type of heat. Let him know I'll cut him in if his paper right." he told Bone

"I'll make sure he gets the message, now back to you, where you going my nigga smelling like Issey Mi." Bone joked. "Bowling" Energy "Where?" he laughed.

"Oh, girl got me meeting her there." Energy "Nigga do you even know how to bowl?" Bone. "Nope, you know me, anything necessary."

Energy had never even step foot in a bowling alley before. He was completely thrown off when they asked for his shoes. There was no way he was wearing shoes someone else had their stinking feet in, so he purchased a brandnew pair for him and Tia. It didn't matter that he may never use them again. They played a few games, but mostly watched everyone else play. They

"SHYNE"

talked most of the date. Enjoying each other's company.

"So, this is what the working-class people do in their spare time?" he asked Tia.

"It's what I like to do." Tia

"So, you gonna let me start occupying your spare time?" he asked

"You know I really didn't think you would come." She said,

"Why not?" he asked,

"You don't seem like the bowling type." She said "So, you asked me thinking I wouldn't come, that's cold."

His phone started to ring, it was Monique. He pushed the silent button. He would take her the car in the morning. He had what he needed.

"What type am I?" he asked,

"You know." She said,

"I don't, that's why I asked." He said,

"You seem to hood for bowling." she said "So, I'm hood, is that how you uppity people think?"

"I'm not uppity. I'm hood like you." she said

"SHYNE"

"You just gotta get to know me. Everybody got a little hood in them" he said,

"I thought that's what we was doing?" she said. His phone started ringing again.

"She knew better" he thought to himself frustrated, like she was the one in the wrong. "Women problems?" she asked

"Bizzness." he said

Tia knew he had to be a dope boy by the way he dressed. The car he drove and the company he kept. Tia was a good girl and good girls love bad boys. He had her right where she wanted to be.

They went back to Tia's studio apartment. Energy thought it was nice and clean. He usually would make his move but, she didn't look like the type that would give it up on the first night, but then she never ran into Energy either.

He made it to Monique's house around 8:00. She was already at work. He took a shower and changed clothes. He felt bad when he saw the unopened champagne bottle on the kitchen table. He knew it was for him. He didn't want Monique, but he didn't want her with anyone else either. He needed her at his disposal when he needed her. Armina texted. (Do you plan on taking care of your son now that you are home. "Really," he laughed. He knew what she wanted and it had nothing to do with his son. (What do you need) he replied. (He starts school this year, can you take me shopping for his school clothes?" She was playing on his weakness. ("I'll send Reagan over with some paper.") he replied.   He wasn't going anywhere near her. It was over, his heart didn't belong to her anymore. She kept texting, asking him why he couldn't bring it himself. He didn't respond. Monique walks through the front door; she was too mad to even look at him. Not mad at him, but mad at herself for being so stupid.

"What's wrong?" he asked as if he didn't know. "I don't understand you." She said. "Fuck you mean, you've known me damn near all your life. Say what's on your mind." He said. "I love you; don't you love me?" she asked

"Hear you go with that dumb shit; you know I love you. I'm a man not a boy, I gotta get this money." He said,

"SHYNE"

"I got money, enough for the both of us." Monique

"I need my own money, I don't expect for nobody to take care of me, baby please don't sweat me damn," he said,

"What about all the stuff you said in your letters." she asked

"What about it? Ain't shit changed its us versus them." He promised

"Whatever?" she said under her breathe. "What?" he asked.

"Nothing, you staying for dinner." Frustrated.

"I'll be back tonight. Rea should be pulling up in a minute to pick me up." They heard her horn blow.

"Don't lie are you coming back or not." She asked.

"I'm coming back" he kissed her forehead. "You ready, what up Nique?" Reagan walked into the house.

"Hey," she said dry as she walked back to her room knowing she wouldn't see him for a while.

"SHYNE"

"Let's go bro," They got into her car.

"So where to, since you past up 5 nice luxury cars for me to drive you around in my raggedy car like I ain't got shit else to do today." Reagan joked. "Shut up girl you don't got no life, I need to go get a car." He said

"For what why don't you keep driving the Lexus into the ground?' she smirked.

"Funny" he smiled "I also need you to do me a favor." he said,

"That is." She said

"Take Armina this change," he handed her a stack of money.

"All this money for what, tell me you ain't tricking off with that-" she was interrupted.
"It's for my son." he said,

"You mean." she asked

"Yeah" he said,

"That nigga gone kill her." She said,

"How he gone find out." he said,

"Damn I got a nephew?" she said

"Keep it on the low, I don't need nothing to happen to them. Not until I can figure this shit out." He knew B-Lo wouldn't step to him but he would kill Armina and his son needed her.

"I'll be discrete I promise," she crossed her heart. "You ain't no damn good. Did you know? Did she tell you?" she asked

"Yeah, she told me." he said,

"What you gonna do?" "Go with the flow right now. I can't do shit. That's the only father he ever known." He said

"You know I got yo back if you need a babysitter or anything." She started laughing to make him laugh.

He purchased an all-money green corvette with white interior. Then he hit the highway to Alabama.

"Nice ride my friend." Ra-Ra.

"Yeah, I call her big booty." Energy

"I see you back so soon." Ra-Ra

"Shit moving quicker than I expected." Energy said.

"Well, you don't want the shit to move slow do you?"

"Shit done changed, it's a whole new game." Energy

"SHYNE"

"Can you handle it? Sound afraid" Ra-Ra. "I ain't afraid of shit" Energy. "Good, how about 20 this go round?" Ra-Ra.

"How about fitty?" Energy. "Fitty it is!" He was impressed with his performance, soon he would have enough to control the south.
$$$$$$$$$$$$$$$$$$$$$$$$$$$$$$$$$$$

A couple months past, Energy and Tia were an item. Tia worked by day and they partied by night. He never went back to Monique's house. Phone calls and texts of broken promises was all the communication they had. He was too busy spoiling Tia and being the ghetto superstar, he was born to be.
 Every women envied Tia as she pulled up to the club driving Energy's brand-new Benz. He sat shotgun. Her best friend Memorie was in the backseat. Summer watched and thought to ruin that little smile off Tia's face and tell her how he fuck with her while she's at work, but she wasn't crazy. Plus, he paid the bills, no need to ruin that.

KARMA

"SHYNE"

Nobody did it bigger than him. He rented out the whole top floor in VIP just for his entourage. He was back on his throne and the whole town knew it. Tia and Memorie were true party girls, turnt up to the max. Unbeknownst to Him Nino was watching him. He was Monique's first cousin and didn't care for him at all. He felt he used Monique to get on and now was acting as if he deserved his crown. He had plans on seeing Energy real soon.

"Look at this clown of a nigga." Nino Said. BLo looked to see who he was talking about. He was pissed. He didn't like the way Energy was making him look like a small-time dealer. Compared to him, he was and always had been. Armina watched as her baby daddy was climbing to the top without her and it piss her off. She didn't care for him. Only the fame and only the fact that he was on top now and that's who she wanted to be with.   B-Lo threw up his glass to salute Energy, he did the same.

"Fuck that boy, he got one time to get wrong and he gonna wish he never left prison." Blo said. "I say

"SHYNE"

"We need to rock that nigga tonight. He gotta have Bone holding the work. I'll get 2 of my young niggas to get at him, say that nigga running through 50 keys a week. I need that shit."
Nino said

"You gotta pick and choose yo battles nigga. This nigga ain't average. You do know that. You can't just send niggas at him all sloppy and shit. You want that nigga, you gotta play by his rules, you gotta be smart." B-Lo

 "I ain't average either nigga, and you need to know that. He just like any other nigga; he bleed like the next man." Nino said,

"I understand that and trust me, I'm with it but to take that nigga, we gonna have to be smart about it." B-Lo

"You must've forgotten I fuck with his sister. All I need to know; I can get from her. Don't be no pussy, you ain't never had a problem robbing a nigga. When I call you, be ready to move."   Nino was ready to take what Energy work hard to get back.

"Memorie!!!" Some dude was yelling over the music, tussling with security to get in Energy's

"SHYNE"

VIP

"Memorie!!!" He kept yelling. It was her crazy on again and off again boyfriend Stacey. He was cussing out security trying to get to her. Energy watched him make a fool of himself for about 5 more minutes and then told them to let him through. He could see he was a hothead, but if he thought he was gonna disrespect him, Energy would put him on his ass. He obviously didn't know the man VIP he was about to disturb.

"Memorie bring yo ass here, don't you hear me calling yo ass." Stacey got in her face not even bothered about Tia and Energy.

"I heard you Stacey, I don't belong to you. You can't just do what you want and think you can show out in public and I'll come back running to you." Memorie and Stacey had a long relationship of cheating and abuse.

"I told you I was sorry about that baby." He said.

"You always sorry, I don't want to hear that shit." she said

"SHYNE"

"You wanna show out in front of these motherfuckers, get yo shit, come on, let's go." He pointed to the exit.

"I'm not going anywhere with you, look at you, you high." She said,

"What bitch?" Stacey had enough of her mouth. Energy had seen enough.

"Calm down my man, have a seat. She ain't ready to go right now." Energy wanted to defuse the situation b-4 he knocked the hell out of him. Stacey looked at him like he had lost his mind, ain't no way this nigga was in his bizzness, and Energy wouldn't've been in it if he hadn't brought it to his door.

"Look man, this here my bitch, MINE she'll go where the hell I tell her." He snatched Memorie arm she jerked away. Energy hated to have to smash him over a bitch. Stacey slapped Memorie so hard, she went deaf. By that time Energy was up from his post and on Stacey's ass. Stacey was trying to match his speed. He really thought he had hands, but he'd never ran into Energy. Memorie and Tia watched as he almost killed Stacey.

"SHYNE"

Tia started screaming for him to stop beating him, as security ran up the stairs. Everyone looking and wondering what was going on up there. Memorie was happy, all the ass whooping she
had gotten, Stacey got what he deserved. Tia grabbed him because security was scared too. They just prayed Stacey wasn't dead.

"Don't touch me, don't you ever fucking touch me, you trying to get killed" he snapped at her. Tia's eyes grew big, didn't recognize this person. Security saw a chance to drag Stacey's body out while Tia had Energy occupied. Thank God he was still breathing.

"I'm sorry." she snap back at him.

"You were going to kill him," seeing her upset brought him back to wherever his mind wondered. Energy knew she was only wanting to help but touching him while he was in beast mode wasn't smart, it was dangerous. Memorie couldn't control the smile creeping in the corners of her mouth. She wanted to hug Energy. Tia walked off mad as hell. "I'll talk to her," Memorie went behind her.

"SHYNE"

The crowd of people we're still looking up to VIP trying to see what the hell just went on. Energy threw his hand up at the D.J. to let him know to start the party back up, and just like that everyone started back dancing. Tia came back with ice wrapped in a towel. She grabbed Energy's swollen hand. He jerked it back from her, he didn't like being treated like a punk he embraced the pain.

"Give me your damn hand." She grabbed it with force throwing the ice on it. He felt relived immediately.

"It's broken" she said.

"It don't feel broke" he said.

"Can you move it" she said with an attitude. He tried

"No" he answered.

"Let's go, I'll fix it up at my house. As they were walking towards the door, Armina made it her bizzness to check on Energy.

"Are you okay?" she asked not bothered about Tia. "Yes." Tia barked, not intimidated. Energy felt the tension.

"SHYNE"

"Tia, Armina, Armina this my girl Tia," Energy only made the situation worst. Armina stormed off.

"The nerve of him introducing that bitch as his girl." She was pissed, she was always and forever supposed to be Energy's girl.

They spent the night at Tia's house. Memorie stayed also, scared to go home not knowing what Stacey would do. Tia bandaged up Energy's hand and gave him pain killers that she often stole from her job to sell on the side. She sold Lortabs, Percocet, you name it.

"What you and Mina got going on?" she asked.

"Where that shit come from? Why you think we got something going on?" he asked nervously

"I saw the look you gave her, the same look you give me." She looked into his eye's demanding the truth. He felt no need to lie to her.

"I used to fuck with her before I went in." "You still fucking her?"

"SHYNE"

"I'm fucking you," he said sincerely.

"I know you fuck with other women; I'm not a fool. Is she one of them?" she asked.

"Nope, how long I got to wear this thing" he changed the subject.

"About 2 weeks," she smiled.

"You gone crazy, how I'm supposed to grip that ass?" He leaned in to kiss her lips.

"I can take care of that." She smiled as they got ready to play.

$$\$$$

Energy purchased a 4- bedroom house a couple blocks from his first home for him and Tia. They spent a lot of time together unless they were working. Of course, he still made time to play in the streets, but he paid the bills. Tia wanted for nothing, she blew her checks on shopping or whatever. Energy was in love all over again.

He pulled up and notice more cars at RaRa's house. It made him suspicious since he never had company over when he visits him. He

"SHYNE"

saw Vittorio Reid, head of one of the Jamaican Cartel, one of the most powerful drug lords in Miami. Energy was almost star struck to be in the same room as him. He heard Ra-Ra talk about him plenty of times but never did he think he would be in his presence. But why was he here at their meeting? Was it good or was it bad?

"Energy I'd like you to meet Vittorio" RaRa. "What up" he shook his hand, still not knowing what the hell was going on.

"You Fam." He said with a thick accent. "Let's take a walk," he told Energy.

Vittorio was dressed in all navy-blue silk Versace. He was brown skin, thick lips, wide nose, short dreads, small eyes, and neatly trimmed facial hairs. They walk out on the back towards the lake.

"So, I hear you are from Mississippi, is this correct?" He asked. Energy nodded.

"You may be wondering why I'm here, so let's just get to it. You move drugs faster than anyone on my team. Certain people have taken a special interest in you. Have you ever heard of a woman by the name of Lisa Michaels?" he asked.

"SHYNE"

Energy nodded no.

"Good, not many people have, but she's a powerful woman and she wants to give you a gift. You will work for me; you will run your own empire in the south, plus a portion in California. I will supply you of course" He told Energy

"What about Ra-Ra, I mean this nigga brought me in." Energy confused   "His time is over and your time is now, think about it, nobody stays on top forever." He explained. What was there to think about, he didn't want to be disloyal to him. He was very thankful for the money he was making, but with Vittorio behind him, he would be a millionaire. What he didn't know was that Ra-Ra was using a lot of product and not meeting his normal quota. Vittorio was tired of explaining what was going on with him. He was sloppy. Energy saved him by moving his product faster than he could use it. Energy didn't sit good with betraying him and taking over, after all he brought him in.

"I don't know if I'm ready for that yet."

"SHYNE"

Energy thinking about the big responsibility of running other cities he didn't live in and knew nothing about.

"Trust me if you wasn't ready, I wouldn't be here. Lisa wouldn't have suggested that I fly to the backwoods to meet you. Think about I'll be in touch." He handed him his card then walked off back towards the house. Energy walked behind him in deep thought. The rest of the visit was cool, they sat around and had drinks and small talked until Vittorio left.

"What did he tell you? What did he ask you to do?" Ra-Ra.

"Shit man why you tripping?" Energy said. "You lying to me, I know Vittorio and that bitch Lisa been wanting to get rid of me. Did they send you to take me out?" He put his gun to Energy's head.

Energy was really confused and this nigga lost his mind pulling a gun on him. He threw up his hands.

"RA YOU TRIPPING NIGGA, I'm your man 100 grand, I wouldn't do no shit like that, get that fucking gun off me." Energy

"SHYNE"

Ra-Ra hesitated, then realizing he was paranoid, lowered his weapon. Energy then grab his gun and pulled it on him.

"Nigga don't ever pull a fucking gun on me. That shit got you tripping. That's why they want to get rid of yo ass. I wasn't gonna move without you, but if you ever play me like that again nigga, Vittorio will be your last fucking worry." Energy snapped

"My bad man." He said,

"Nigga fuck you, I'm out." he walk towards the exit.

"Leave then nigga, just remember, who you work for. I started this shit. I brought you in. You remember that." he yelled.

Energy left pissed off, he had decisions to make. Things to think about, he didn't want to cut his man out, but was afraid he may have to kill him. When he got back home, he went to the barber shop for a haircut.

"What up Fam?" he said to his barber Chris.

"What up, I got one in front of you," He told Energy. He nodded, then took a seat in the waiting area. The neighborhood kids started running in behind him. Every time they seen his car anywhere, they would come running. He loved kids and he loved feeling like Robinhood to them.

"You still the same," B-lo walked in with his son to get a haircut.

"I ain't gonna never change." Energy said, "I saw you smash Stacey the other night, that nigga always on some bull, that's why I hardly fuck with him." He told Energy. Which was strange. Memories told him they were cousins and were really close. He figured he was on some beef.

"I been wanting to holla at you on some grown man shit." B-Lo said.

"Spill it," really not wanting to hear it.

"What you getting them thangs for, I would get a lot more if I could get em a little cheaper." B-Lo said.

"Nigga how you sound, everybody would get a lot more if they could get em cheaper." Energy explained

"SHYNE"

"I got 200k to spend right now, I just wanted to know if you would lower it for me this one time?" he asked.

"Where they do that at, next you'll be asking to meet my connect." He frowned.

B-Lo was embarrassed, but he shouldn't've expected anything less from him. It was no secret how they felt about each other, Energy could have lowered his price especially since he was about to cut out the middleman.

"It's like that nigga. I'm just trying to eat." B-Lo said.

"So, you ain't eating?" Energy motioning with his hands. "Nawl nigga you greedy" Energy spat.

If B-Lo wasn't pissed, he was pissed now. He was sick of Energy treating him like a little boy.

"I'm trying to get paid, and you trying to keep a nigga under you, I ain't made to be under no man." B-Lo said

"You saying this to say what? I ain't forced you to shop with me. I gave you a price, you jumped on it, I'm guessing it was clearly cheaper then ya man's cause you stop shopping with him

"SHYNE"

and started shopping with me. Now if you want, you are more than welcome to go back and shop with him. I ain't gonna starve." Energy said arrogantly. He knew he was pushing him but he didn't give a fuck.

"You right fam, I know what this really about." B-Lo felt the need to belittle him right back. "Mina" he said with force behind his voice. "This nigga had to be high" Energy thought. "You pissed about Mina" he raised his voice.

"You need to stay off that shit my nigga." Energy trying not to get upset.

"You mad because I got a son by yo girl?" He got cocky. Everyone started turning their attention towards them.

"My girl, that's what's wrong with you now, wanting to be Energy, but there can only be one me. She's not my girl. I thought she was your girl." Energy was still calm letting him know he had showed his hand.

"Wanting to be you, how the fuck you sound, you see that" he pointed outside the window. "The sun rises and sets on my ass, nigga. I been running this motherfucker, who the fuck is you nigga? I been getting money." B-Lo got really arrogant, he didn't care that he needed him. His prices were a lot cheaper, but energy wasn't about to make a fool of him in public.

"She was your girl until I took her." B-Lo.

"I was gone to the Pen; she was anybody's bitch. What you want brownie points for sleeping with my seconds, ok nigga you won, but since you want to taste my dick so badly, I'll let you in on a little secret. You see that little nigga right there," he pointed to his son in the barber chair.

"He's mine too," Energy let his ego get the best of him. There was no way he should've said what he said, but he couldn't take it back now.

B-Lo's heart almost stop as he looks into his son's eyes and for the first, he realized they weren't his own. Energy won again and he felt like a complete fool. Everyone in the barber shop pretended not to hear his last comment. B-lo walks in slow motion grabbing his son out the chair with his haircut half-finished. He walked out the door defeated. He wanted to shoot Energy in the face, but there were way too many witnesses. Tears stream down his face as he called Nino.

"SHYNE"

"Spit it before ya forget it." He answered.
"We move on that nigga tonight! "B-Lo yelled
"Tonight?" Nino asked.

"Tonight." B-Lo

"What happened I thought you said-" He
was interrupted. "Tonight nigga" he yelled and
hung up the phone.

Energy couldn't sleep at all that night. He
shouldn't have let B-Lo push his buttons. He
didn't know what kind of danger he had put
Armina and his son in. If anything happened to
them, he wouldn't forgive himself, knowing it was
his fault. "Hello" he answered his phone happy to
hear Armina's voice. He knew she would be
calling after what went down at the Barber shop.
"What the FUCK was you thinking." She said
through clinched teeth.

"I'm sorry mane, I wasn't" he tried to plead
his case. "He took my son. He said he'll kill him if I
call the police" she started crying. He panic
throwing on his clothes

"Took him where?" he asked

"SHYNE"

"If I knew I wouldn't be calling you, this is all your fucking fault, my baby is gone. Please find mine baby?" she started screaming at him.

He hung up the phone. He couldn't think with her screaming, but she was right, this was his mess, and because of his ego he endangered his son. He prayed B Lo wasn't stupid, if he hurt his son, he planned to make everyone he knew suffer. Energy stepped out his front door and was hit in the head with a pistol. Blood immediately started leaking from his head.

"Get back in the house nigga," one of the young boys forced him back into the house.

"Where yo bitch at?" the other robber asked. "Ain't nobody here," he said. Tia was working nights this week thank God, but how did they know someone else would be there. They sounded like kids he thought to himself. The two gunmen had their face covered, one had long dreads which was stupid in committing a robbery.

"Where it at nigga, you know what the fuck we want" one of them cocked the gun in his face. One false move he could lose his life to one of these hotheaded youngsters. He decide to give

"SHYNE"

them what they wanted. He walk them down to the basement. He had no intention on dying and no plans on the kids leaving the basement alive, he got to the last step and quickly hit the light switch.

"What the fuck happen? Where he go?" before he could get an answer, a bullet pierced his skull. The other young boy was frighten in the pitch-black basement; he felt the steel against his head.

"Who sent you? "Energy asked

"Aight, aight it was B-Lo He said to rob you and kill you. B-Lo wants you dead. That's it, that's all, please don't kill me." the young boy plead for his life.

"B-Lo sent you at me?" he almost laughed. "Yea, Yea, B-Lo." The youngster said.

Energy knew he had to have been stupid to send kids at him. He would've respected him more if he would've came himself.

He decided to negotiate with the young man in exchange for his life.

"SHYNE"

"I'm gonna let you go" He said. The kid was relieved. "Call and tell him, its done and you go free." Energy said,
"That's it?" young boy. "That's it." Energy put his gun away.   The young boy put the call in to B-Lo and told him he had 40 bricks and 169 thousand in cash and jewelry. Energy walked towards the stairs, the kid followed behind at the top of the stairs, Energy turn and shot him twice in the head. His body tumble back to the bottom of the stairs.

He headed to Bone's house with both kids cell phone's on him. He started beating down the door soon as he got there. "Bone" he was yelling through the door.

"What is it dawg?" a sleepy Bone unlocked the door. He was quickly awaken when Energy snatched him out into the cold.

"B-Lo gotta die tonight. That nigga tried to have me killed. I got 2 dead bodies back at my place, and B-Lo got my son," he screamed in his face.

"Son, what the fuck you talking about." He thought he was delusional.

"SHYNE"

"I'll explain later, right now I need a cleanup crew at my crib and you to find someone to trace this last call. That nigga think I'm dead, well welcome to the mother fucking after life." Energy spat

"Let me make a few calls and grab Lucille" Bone said as they walked back into the house. Their source tracked the guys to Stacey house.

"That's the house?" Energy asked as he cut off the lights. They were a short distance down the street. "Yep," Bone cocked his pistol. Energy wasted no time, he peeped in the front window. B-Lo and Stacey were both seated on the sofa. A plate of cocaine was on the table and also 2 guns. He saw his son asleep on the couch next to them, he was relieved to see his chest rise and fall, but B-Lo had committed the ultimate. There was no way he would let him live to see tomorrow. Stacey and B-Lo was so high they wouldn't have noticed if Energy were standing in the room with them. He could hear them deep in conversation.

"She told me, the bitch said it out her on mouth. I been taking care of this nigga son, another nigga's son, ain't that some shit. Them motherfuckers played me fam. I tried to kill that bitch." B-Lo said.

"Mane that's fucked up, you know I can't stand that bitch ass nigga, so I'm with whatever you with." Stacy still salty over the beat down Energy gave him.

"That nigga gone bruh, I told em not to fuck with me, plus I

got the dope and the money. Nino scared to send his niggas so I sent my own. It's over the streets are mine." B-Lo thinking he had killed Energy

"What you gonna do with shorty" Stacey pointed to his son asleep on the couch.

"I just wanted to scare her up, I knew she would call that nigga and he would come running. I had some of my young nigga's waiting outside his house to handle that business." He grab his gun off the table high as hell wanting to imitate the robbery.

"I told that nigga I was gonna fuck him up" still waving gun around. "Stop waving that damn pistol nigga." Stacy hit another line from the plate, as the door flew open, B-Lo got spook, he tried to aim, if he wasn't high, he might've gotten a shot off in the right direction. Instead, he shot Stacy in the head. Energy put 3 bullets threw B-Lo's chest. Bone grab Energy's son off the couch so they could leave. Energy paused. Bullets started flying through the window. Nino was sitting outside watching everything unfold. They hit the ground covering Energy's son as the house fell under attack. Energy looked up to see were the fire was coming from. "Stay down, I'm going out the back." He yelled to Bone.

He made his way out a side window and opened fire as the young men fled the scene. He had no idea who they were or what was going on. He figured his family was in danger, he called Reagan and Tia and gave them instructions not to leave the house for a few days. Bone came out with his son when he saw it was safe.

Armina had been pacing the floor all night. Energy hadn't answered her calls since she told him about their son being kidnap. She was about to call the police when she heard footsteps on her porch. She swung open the door and cried as she saw Bone carrying her son. He was shook up and happy to see his mother. She held him tight thanking God for returning him to her safely. Energy noticed the black eyes and dried-up blood around her lip. He hated himself for letting his emotions guide his feelings. He never meant to put her or his son in harm's way.

Armina was so mad, she couldn't even look at him. She was thankful for him bringing back her son but wasn't ready to forgive him. She slammed the door in his face.

$$$$$$$$$$$$$$$$$$$$$$$$$$$$$$

Energy went to surprise Tia at work.

"Latia Laurence please," he ask the lady at the front desk, who paged Tia.

"Energy," Monique said as she walked up closer to him. Dressed in her white coat holding her clip board. She hadn't heard from him in weeks, now here he was in her place of work. Energy was slightly embarrassed, him and Monique played this game and he knew he would eventually fuck with her again, but this was about to be awkward.   "How you been?" Was all he could come up with.

"SHYNE"

"I've been ok and you?" Monique was confused as to why he was there?

"Yea I been chilling," he said nervously, know shit was about to blow up in a moment.

"What are you doing here?" She wanted to know, but before he could answer, Tia popped up grabbing his waist from behind.

"Hey babe, what you doing here?" Tia asked. Monique was wanting to know the same thing.

"I'm taking you to lunch" he said. Hoping she didn't see them talking. Monique was growling angry.

"How sweet, I see you meet the boss lady." She introduced Monique.

"Yeah, I did." He answered. Monique was near tears. Of all the women, why he chose her, she had way more to offer then Tia. Monique was gritting her teeth. She was so mad; how did Tia end up with her man? She must've been the reason he hadn't been around.

"Let me go grab my things." A jolly Tia said walking off.

"SHYNE"

"Look Nique" he tried to plead his case. "Save it, same ol song we both grown now, no need to go there." She said.

"I didn't know you worked here." He said. "You didn't know because you didn't want to know. Don't worry, I'll stay in the shadows as always, it's your world." She walked off.

Energy felt like shit, he would never disrespect her like that, not on purpose anyway. Monique watched as they walked out the door. Tia going on and on about her day. Energy pretended to be listening, his mind wondering as he looked back at Monique.

Later that night Monique called Reagan to fill her in about the latest Energy madness.

"He's fucking one of my employees." She told Reagan

"No way" Reagan said but, knew it was true.

"Yes girl, you could imagine the shock when he saw me, lets you know he doesn't do his homework or he would've known she works with me." she chuckled to keep from crying. "I wonder does he know the bitch like women too." Monique said.

"She's gay. "Reagan asked.

"Straight like that, she got a girl she goes out to lunch with almost 3 times a week and the bitch never comes back on time, everybody knows that's her girlfriend. This shit is crazy." Monique said.

"Hell, his ass doesn't care, the more the merrier." She just didn't understand how Monique could still love Energy after all the hell he put her through. All the women, all the back and forth.

"Let me call you back" Monique said. She heard her front door open. Reagan was the only other person besides Energy who had a key so she knew exactly who it was. Energy was home like it was the right thing to do. The incident at the hospital made him miss her, not that he needed her, just the sex.
She walked into the kitchen to see him rummaging through her refrigerator.

"Your hoe don't feed ya." She snapped
"You gonna play those games with me" he smiled.

"SHYNE"

"You ready to playhouse again" she rolled her eyes.

"I ain't come here for all that." He said.

"What the fuck I'm supposed to say, you leave here for weeks, then show back up like it was yesterday." She said.

"I'm here ain't I." he said.

"For how long" Monique. "Don't do this Nique." He said

"No, don't you do this, yo ass feeling guilty." She said

"We're not together, I don't got shit to feel guilty about." He handed her a stack of money. "What's this?" She ask.

"100 thousand" he said proudly. "I-knowthat-much. I can see the bands around it. What's it's for?" she said with attitude.

'Interest" he said.

"So, you treating me like a whore, let's get one thing straight, money don't impress me. I'm not a gold digger, I got money." She said.

"Then give it back" he smiled. That smiled made her forget her words. All she wanted was for him to stay and never leave again.

KARMA

"SHYNE"

"I ain't giving you shit," she said. "stop playing, I'm hungry." He said. "Why your dyke ain't feeding you," she mumbled under her breath.

"What?" not understandig what she said. "How come you didn't know where your girl works." She said.

"I knew where she works, I just didn't know you worked there." He said.

"So, you didn't know where I worked at." She said.

"You do realize I been locked up. No, I don't know where you work. I'm sorry about that shit, I would've even came in if I knew you worked there." He said.

"So, I guess you know everything you need to know about Tia huh?" she sassed.

Energy knew she was hiding something. "Why you say it like that?" he asked.

"So, you let a bitch have you so sprung that you can't even call me to say hi, how you doing today, call to say fuck you or nothing." What she really wanted to say was "What Tia has, that she didn't."

"SHYNE"

"I'm not sprung." He said. "I don't blame you, since she like what you like." Monique said sarcastically. He wanted to laugh in her face. She thought he didn't know Tia was a bisexual. Tia told him long ago. In fact, he had sex with her and her best friend Memorie and other woman on several occasions. She got off by watching him with other women.

"That's her business so are you gonna fix me something to eat or what?" he asked Seeing she had no room to hate on Tia, she fixed him up a good meal followed by good sex like always. She fell asleep in his arm's; the world was once again perfect. To her surprise, he was still there the next morning. Tia had went back home for a family reunion that weekend. So, he chilled too late in the afternoon. She was glad to have him back with her, even if it was a lie.

$$$$$$$$$$$$$$$$$$$$$$$$$$$$$

Bone pulled up to the trap house in his Audi S8. His money was looking good now that he was second in charged. He just purchased a new condo for his aunt. He was dropping off a package to the twins. The twins ran the trap house. They were 17-year-old boys, identical, light skin, medium build with long dreads. He nominated them to Energy because they had proven themselves as pit bulls in the streets.

"What's up boys?" Bone said to the boys. Tonio and Ace just nodded as they continue to play the Xbox, bone threw the duffle bag with 15 bricks on the table.

"I'll whoop yo ass later. Gotta get this money right now," Tonio said as he got up to cook the dope.

"Yeah, I hear ya, you betta pay me my damn money." His brother joked still playing the game. "Where the hell you been? You done had me on hold all day. I hope this still the good shit." Tonio said.

"Nothing but the best." Bone.

"That's my dawg," Tonio gave him dap.

"Come on bruh, off yo ass and on yo feet. We need to get this paper." Tonio told Ace who was still playing the game. "Hold up one minute" Ace still playing.

"SHYNE"

"Get the fuck up nigga, time don't wait for no man, and check that   door, make sure the deadbolt lock" Bone spat.

"Aight mane paranoid ass, why the fuck you ain't lock the dam deadbolt?" Walking to the door to check it. When the door came flying off the hinges, 4 armed men in black came through the door.

"Get the fuck down, don't play crazy, y'all know what the fuck it is." They had guns in there face before Bone could react.

"Fuck," he said aloud.

"Check em for guns" one of the robbers said as he pushed him down to the floor. Bone was trying to get a look at their eyes since that was all he could see. If they let him live revenge would be of the essence.

"Put all that shit in the bag make them niggas empty his pockets too." Robber #1.

Everyone face down as the robbers sped through the house taking money, dope,   or whatever they could find.

"What the fuck you looking at?" Robber #1 said to Bone. He had something in his mouth

"SHYNE"

disguising his voice. Bone looked down at the floor. "That's right nigga, eat the flo." He kicked him in the face. "Let's go" another robber ran out the house. "Thanks for your time gentlemen." Robber #1 said as all of them ran out the house fast as they came.

Everyone eased up from the floor, not believing what just happened. Bone was rubbing his head in frustration. He snatched Ace up.

"Nigga, I told you to lock the fucking door." Bone.

"How the fuck was I supposed to know, we was finna get hit." Ace pleaded.

"Yo mane chill," Tonio pulled him from his brother.

"Chill, Chill, you know what the fuck Energy gone do, when he finds out, the money and dope gone." Bone said.

"Energy got plenty mo spots, this shit apart of the game. My nigga" Tonio said.

"Well tuff guy you call the nigga and tell em, all I know is this spot here nobody supposed to know about. So, either a mother fucker been watching me or y'all." He pointed to them. "Either way he don't give a fuck." Bone spat as they look nervously as Bone called Energy.

"I was just about to call you" Energy answered.

"We got a problem" Bone said,

"We always do" Energy said sarcastically.

"Our spot just got hit." He said,

"You mean my spot." Energy tried to remain calm.

"Which spot?" he asked.

"Monroe," Bone said. Energy sighed. Monroe was his main spot, no one knew about it but him Bone and the twins.

"How much?" he asked.

"Enough." Bone answered.

"I'm on my way." Everyone was silent as Energy walked around examining the house like a detective on CSI.

"Where were you at again?" he asked Tonio who hated the interrogation.

"I told you already" he answered frustrated.

"SHYNE"

"And I'm asking you again nigga. SPEAK" Energy.

Tonio sighed. "I was about to cook the dope. That's when the door came down." His heart beating 100mph. He felt as if he would faint if Energy asked him one more question. Energy watched their body language as they each told the story.

"So, nobody got a look at these dudes?" Energy running out of patience.

"We couldn't see their faces, they had on masks" Ace spoke up. Energy was really cool which made everyone else nervous. They were expecting their bodies to drop at any moment.

"Let's get back to work, I'll have Bone to bring some bricks over in the morning, y'all did good." Energy left out the house Bone close behind.   Bone was really confused; he knew Energy didn't play. Something was up, plus he didn't take loses, he made it perfectly clear if his house got hit, the loss is yours. You get the money back or pay the debt with your life.

"Yo mane, we gonna put in overtime to get this paper-" Bone tried pleading.

"SHYNE"

"They're lying" Energy.

"I was right there with them." Bone.

"They know who they are." He said.

"You think they that stupid." Bone said. "Not them, but somebody is, I want you to keep an eye on them, I'm not ready to kill them yet. They gonna lead me to my dope first." Energy cut his eyes at Bone in a way to let him know the conversation was over and he could exit the car.

Bone didn't know what to believe. He hope that Energy was just being paranoid. He trusted the twins and prayed they hadn't betrayed him. Energy was a dangerous man, he prayed for all their sake. They had better sense then to cross him.

$$$$$$$$$$$$$$$$$$$$$$$$

Tia was in the bathroom stall at work holding a positive pregnancy test in her hand. She wasn't ready to be a mother and she knew it. Plus, Energy had enough baby mama drama going on with Armina. Ever since B-Lo was found dead, she let the world know that Energy was her child's father.

"SHYNE"

"Tia, you ok" Monique said. Tia had been in the bathroom for a while. She could hear her sobbing in the stall.

"Yeah," she walked out with the test in her hand. Monique heart almost stop as she looked down at the pregnancy test, she took a deep breathe. "Is that?" She asked.

"Yes" Tia wiped her eyes. It took everything in Monique to stand up straight. She had to remain professional. Energy made it a religion that they use condoms. If he hadn't made her have an abortion, she would've had his first child not Armina.

"Are you gonna be ok, I really need to go" Monique said. Tia shook her head yes as Monique left out full speed. She had to get out of there before she screamed. Her heart ached so badly, she felt sick to her stomach. She wanted answers.
She dialed his number.

"Talk to me" he answered. Monique was yelling and crying, he couldn't understand anything she was saying.

"SHYNE"

"Girl you better speak fucking English or I'm about to hang up this damn phone" Energy. "She's pregnant" Monique yelled "Who?" he asked.

"Tia, she's fucking pregnant." She said. "What the fuck you talking about?" he was confused. "You made me have an abortion, then you go get two bitches pregnant," Monique was still yelling and going off.

Energy hung up the phone in her face. She kept calling back, he didn't answer. He dialed Tia's number; she didn't answer. So, he texted her 911.

"What's the emergency?" she sounded normal as ever. "I need you to come home." He said.

"Now?" she asked.

"Yeah." He said.

"I'll see if I can leave, is there something wrong?" she asked,

"I just need to see you." He lied "Give me an hour."

Energy was in deep thought. Not knowing if he was ready to bring another life into the world. They were in love with each other, but they still did their share of dirt. Energy sleep with other women and so did she. They were living a wild and lavish life and they loved it. Energy was enough man for her, but he could never curve her appetite for women. Their sexual lifestyle made their relationship stronger. Tia never planned on getting pregnant.

"Hey babe" she kissed his lips and straddle him on the couch. He grabbed her around her waist as he always did.

"You feeling ok." He asked,

"Good as ever, what's up?" Tia wanting to know the reason he had her leave work.

"Are you pregnant?" he just came out with it. "What the fuck," she thought to herself this was really weird and awkward. She didn't even know what she was gonna do with the baby. She was leaning on having an abortion, but thanks to Monique telling Energy she had to confess. No way she was lying to him, she knew he was a border line psycho.

"SHYNE"

"Yes, how do you know?" she asked confused. "When were you going to tell me?" ignoring her question.

"Hell, I just found out, you must be physic or something. I was in the bathroom; my boss came in." She paused for a minute remembering a time she thought she walked up on the two of them engaging in a conversation. The day that he surprised her at work. Energy was smart but not that smart. He was watching her eyes reading her thoughts. They slept with other people but not her boss.

"You fucking Monique." She jumped up. "Are you stupid?" he said.

"Hell nawl, motherfucker, but you think I am, she was the only person that knew. You fucked with a lot of bitches, but my boss, really, out of all the hoes in the world, you go fuck that ugly bell pepper shaped bitch." She spat Energy was embarrassed.

"What the fuck did I say?" He jumped in her face.

"SHYNE"

"Ok we can settle this shit right now." She pulled out her phone to call Monique which was a waste of time. Monique knew not to say a word. She didn't answer.

"How the fuck did I miss this shit. You already knew her, I thought I saw some weird shit the day I introduced y'all," she threw up quotation marks with her hands. "Reagan is your sister, she calls her best friend Rae, you got this bitch laughing at me behind my back, while she fucking my man. I know about all the other hoes you sleep with, why I didn't know about Ms. Piggy? tell me why?" Tia was up pacing the floor pissed off, pointing her fingers in his face.

"You betta calm yo ass down before I slap the fuck out of you." Energy.

"Tell me I'm lying," Tia not threaten by his comment. He didn't speak.

"What I thought." She said,

"It's complicated, we grew up together yes."

He was interrupted.

"SHYNE"

"Why the hell you ain't been said nothing, cause you lowdown, running around fucking my boss behind my back." She said,

"There's nothing to tell." He explained

"I'm about to lose my job." She said

"No, you're not." He assured her

"Ima beat that bitch ass, watch." She said.

Energy decide to let her vent, he couldn't get a word in anyway and he would hate to knock her out pregnant or not. Monique called her phone back.

"You a snake ass bitch" she answered. Monique knew she must've found out about Energy. She remained professional but was smiling wide inside.

"If I didn't think you were the best in the state, I would fire you for that comment. Now what seems to be the problem?" Monique still smiling inside, she was finally winning.

"Don't play with me bitch" Tia irritated. "Fuck you I quit." She said.

"Don't be stupid, this is your career. You think he's going to take care of you the rest of your life, and you're having a baby." Monique sarcastically. Tia hung up in her face. She hated to admit it but Monique was right. She had to think of herself.

"I'm having an abortion." She didn't trust him. She had a future to protect. She went in the room slamming the door. Energy gave her time to cool off. She is talking out her head.

Never a dull moment, conflict after conflict. He thought as he called Reagan.

"What's good bruh" Reagan answered. "Where you at?" he asked her

"Spending the money, you gave me" she said. He laughed; he spoiled her rotten.

"Glad I could make someone happy today." He said

"You always do, what's up with your ass?" She could her the disgust in is voice.

"Shits all fucked up Monique, man. Armina getting all my damn nerves and Tia wants to have an abortion." He explained

"I told you so," Is what she was thinking, but she knew her brother needed someone to talk to. Even if he wasn't gonna take her advice.

"SHYNE"

She still enjoyed their talks.

"What you gonna do?" she asked.

"I don't know what to do, I need a vacation." He said,

"I'm down, you know that" they shared a laugh. "I'll let you know, how is Unc?" he asked. "You already know." She answered.

"Yeah, I do, so what's up with you and what's his name." he asked,

"I broke up with him." She said. "Sorry to hear that," he said sarcastically.

"Yeah right. He ain't bout shit, keep asking me to hook him up with you." She said "For what?" he ask.

"What you think, he had become obsessed." She said,

"Why the hell you didn't tell me Rae?" He asked,

"Wasn't no need, I knew you wouldn't fuck with him, you can't stand him." Reagan was only book smart when it came to the streets, she was clueless.

"Let me call you back" he hung up annoyed.

"SHYNE"

"Bone meet me in an hour, I know who hit my spot" Energy put two and two together. Nino either robbed him or he know who did, either way he was a dead man.

"What's up fam?" Bone gave Energy dap as he got in the car.

"Nino," he said

"You sho" Bone didn't think so he was the one who told him he was harmless.

"I told you I didn't like that nigga. He couldn't get to me so he must've started watching you." He pointed to him.

"SO, you think he's the mastermind behind the robbery?" Bone thought he was foolish, but he was about to find out how wrong he was. "Yep, and we going to pay him a visit." Energy said

"I'm with you fam." Bone

It was 10:30 at night and they were sitting up the street from Nino apartment. Watching the traffic go in and out

. "What the fuck we waiting for?" Bone impatiently.

"SHYNE"

"That," Energy pointed at the red Lexus truck. Bone's mouth flew wide open.

"You still think I'm paranoid?" Energy asked Bone as they watched the twins go into Nino's apartment.

"Shit don't mean nothing" Bone defensibly. "We about to find out." Energy said Now it was Bone who was paranoid, he had introduced the twins to Energy, he said they could be trusted. If they had betrayed that trust he knew Energy would kill him with a blink of an eye.

He was sweating bullets as they walked down the street to the run-down apartment building. The neighborhood kids had knocked out most the streetlights with rocks. They kicked in the door.

Nino started shooting first they returned fire as he ran in the back room. Ace open fire, Bone shot him in the stomach.

 Tonio fled to the back.

"You stole from me?" Energy stood over Ace body. Ace didn't say a thing, he held his bleeding stomach.

"SHYNE"

"Have it your way" he put 2 shots in his head. Bone was dragging Tonio into the front, pistol held to his head. "Nino jumped out the window." Bone told him.

"From up here?" Energy surprised, they were 6 floors up.

"Man, please don't kill me" Tonio pleaded for his life.

"Shut up nigga, I trusted you." Bone.

"It wasn't me, it was Nino" he cried when he saw his brothers dead body, he loved his brother and really didn't want to live anymore. He knew he was a dead man. He hoped they would make it quick
. "Where's my dope?" he asked.

"It's in the back" he said. Energy nodded for Bone to check the back.

"It's not all here, it's about 20" he yelled from the back.

"That's it?" Energy asked. He didn't answer. "Not enough" he sent a bullet through his head.

Bone came from the back with the bricks, he met Energy's gun. Energy put 4 shots in his

Chest. Energy grabbed the bricks and left the apartment. He had no tolerance for errors in is army. Bone would pay for his mistakes with his life. There was no sign of Nino when he came out, so he would put a bounty on his head, soon he would be dead.

$$\$$$

3 months past and no one had saw Nino. Word was he left town.

Monique was determined not to be the side chick anymore. She had enough there was no way Tia would be the only one having his baby. It made her sick every time she saw her around the office, her belly starting to poke out a bit. Monique was trying to get pregnant. She knew if she had his child, he wouldn't have any other choice but to stay, that's what their relationship needed. She been tampering with the condoms the last couple times they hooked up.

Energy trusted her so the condoms always stayed at her house. She was getting ready to leave work when Energy called her for a late-night rendezvous. She prayed he really was coming, he often stood her up and she needed to get pregnant. She received a page from Dr. Ramsey. She was the head doctor over Monique.

"Hello Dr," She answered her office phone.

"Hi Monique, can you stop by my office on your way out please?" Dr. Ramsey

"Sure, I'm on my way down," Monique was worried. They just took yearly physicals 2 days ago. She hope everything was ok.

"Have a seat please" She told her. Monique was a doctor also so she knew in her tone something was wrong.

"I'll stand," she looked around the room for any clues to tell her why she was there. "Is everything ok?" Monique asked,

" I'm sorry to tell you but your blood work was abnormal." Dr. Ramsey

"I don't understand abnormal how." She asked

"You tested positive for H.I.V." The room feel silent, she could see her lips moving, but she couldn't make out the words. She started crying, placing her head in her hands.

"SHYNE"

"It's gonna be ok" Doctor Ramsey tried to comfort her.

"H.I.V." she yelled
"I have your papers right here; you know it's not a death sentence anymore. People are living normal lives with H.I.V. The most important thing is that we contact your sexual partners."

Monique only had one partner. Who didn't even know he was having unprotected sex. Monique felt sick as she thought about the fact that she did this to herself. Tampering with the condoms that were designed to protect her. Is that the reason he made sure they used condoms? How long had he known? Did he even know? Her thoughts running 100mph.   "I'll give you a little time, do you need me to drive you home?" She asked her. She didn't say a word, she walked out like a zombie. Not even looking back. She didn't even know how she made it home. Her life was over, she was dying. She went to her liquor cabinet. She never used it for nothing but decoration. She drowned herself in a bottle of Grey Goose. She was devastated.

"SHYNE"

"The dirty, no good, infected ass motherfucker. It's all his fault. I let that bastard ruin my life. I'm a doctor and now look at me, I'm supposed to know better." She let the liquor talk to her, she made a phone call, and then cried herself to sleep.

Everything was his fault.

"Yo Nique" she heard Energy's voice yelling through the house around 6:30 the next morning. Her stomach cringe at his voice. She wanted to throw up in disgust. Her chested tighten up. He found her in the bedroom. "You been drinking damn what's wrong?" he saw the empty bottle of Grey Goose. He knew she doesn't drink so something definitely was wrong.   "It's always something," he thought and he normally played a big part. She burst into tears then pulled a gun from under her pillow. She was hungover and not clearly thinking. All she knew is that she was dying. She loved Energy, but he had to pay." They would die together, she thought. Energy was a sitting duck. His pistol was in the car, he never had a need for it in her house. If he had it on him, she would already be dead.

"SHYNE"

"Are you going fucking crazy bitch, put the gun away. What the fuck is wrong with you?" He didn't know what state of mind she was in or what had her so upset. Maybe she was still mad about the baby. He thought to overpower her and take the gun and beat her to death with it, but this was Monique, she wouldn't dare hurt him. She's just mad.

"I'm H.I.V. positive" she yelled at him still pointing the gun. Energy's face was stoned. This was serious.

"What the fuck did you say?" starring down the barrel of the gun, confused on why it was his fault. They always used protection and if what she was saying was true then he's glad he did.

"You let a nigga give you H.I.V." he said, "You motherfucker, you did this to me." she snapped.

"I ain't gave you shit. Are you losing your mind, we use rubbers? Now you got 5 seconds to put down the gun or its not gonna be good. I'm telling you and I'm about to fuck you up." He was

"SHYNE"

dead serious; he had played her game long enough.

"Fuck you, I hate you. I hate I ever fucking loved you. You never gave a fuck about me." she yelled.

"Hell, nawl bitch, and I ain't gonna tell you again, get that gun out my fucking face." He yelled

"What about this gun nigga," Nino had the gun to the back of his head. Monique called her cousin and gave him the rundown. She agreed to trap Energy in the house for Nino to kill him. She wanted him dead, she wanted him to pay. Energy couldn't believe she of all people had done this to him. He always knew death was coming for him, but not at the hands of a women scorned. He looked into Monique's eyes searching them for any signs of remorse. Nino sent 2 shots through his head. His body dropped immediately.

Monique started to panic, what had she done, she forgotten she had called her cousin. She knew they hated each other plus, he got a bounty on his head so it was a win for him. Seeing energy dead brought her back to reality. She didn't want him dead anymore.

"Come on cuz, we need to get out of here," Nino told her but she wasn't listening.

"Energy," she screamed running to his side. "What have you done?" she started screaming at Nino crying over Energy's body. Blood covered her hands making her hysterical.

"Come on baby, stay with me, don't leave." She said holding his head, blood dripped from his mouth. Nino was confused as hell; she had called him for this reason. "I'm sorry baby. I'm so sorry. I didn't mean to hurt you." She kissed his lips and closed his eyes. He was dead, the man she loved all her life had died by her doing.

"Come on cuz" Nino told her.

"Fuck you, fuck you, you killed him," she started yelling at him. He decided that she was delusional. Either way, she couldn't be trust. A single bullet ended her life. Nino fled the scene in Monique's car.

The house was silent as Dr, Ramsey voice came across the answering machine. "Monique if your home pick up please, its Dr. Ramsey."

"SHYNE"

Monique laid lifeless with her eyes wide open. "Monique, I'm terribly sorry, there's been some sort of mix up with your blood work. I know you were real upset that's why I'm calling. Please, if your home pick up your test was a false positive. Your blood work is normal in fact you're having a baby. Your 6 weeks pregnant. Please call me asap I apologize once again."

EULOGY

Reagan sat quietly on the front pew. She hadn't spoken in two days. Her uncle and nephew sat beside her. Armina and Tia also seated up front. The whole city came out to pay their respect to the ghetto super star. Lisa Michael's paid for his funeral. She had also sent Reagan a nice amount of cash. Everyone knew how much he loved his sister. She was his reason for living.

Ra-Ra was in attendance, he also gave Reagan cash and told her if there was anything she needed, he was a call away but she didn't need anything but Energy. She lost both her best friends. 4 hours after Nino left, he was pulled over for running a stop sign in Georgia. He had blood on him and guns in the car. He admitted to police he had killed his cousin and her boyfriend but only at her request. Phone records proved they had spoken before the murders. Reagan didn't want to believe it until the police played a tape of Monique saying she wanted Energy dead, but Nino would never make it to court. He was found dead in his cell hours after his confession.

Monique was buried 2 hours earlier; Reagan attended the wake but did not attend the funeral. She loved Monique but hated her for taking away her heart. Reagan starred at her nephew, he looked just like his father. Tia's son would be born in a couple months. Reagan would now be

"SHYNE"

all alone in the world. She lost the most important people in her life. What would she do without Energy? Her whole body was just numb. At least when he was away in prison, she could still visit and talk with him. Tears stream down her face as she pictured his charming smile, a smile she would surely miss,

Everyone in attendance turn to the beautiful light skin women that walked through the church doors. Her long grey hair all way down her back. Reagan recognized her immediately even without the handcuffs and shackles or the correctional officers who stood guarding the door. She hadn't saw her since she was 6 year's old. She was still as beautiful as the morning she drop her off at school and didn't return. Reagan didn't even look up as she walked past her to Energy's casket. Tears rolled down her face. Her son was dead before his 30th birthday. This was her Karma. She'd taken someone's son, now someone had taken her son.

KARMA

COMING SOON :

THICKER THAN

BLOOD II

KARMA

"SHYNE"

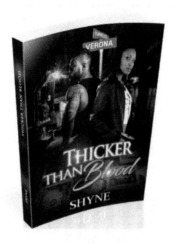

NOW AVAILABLE ORDER copy at
thehairmadam.com. also available on AMAZON

KARMA

"SHYNE"

About The Author

Nakisha "Shyne" Neal is a Chicago native but was raised in Mississippi. Where she lives with her husband and 5children. When she is not working on her next book, she is a beautician hard at work at the hair salon. She enjoys taking trips with her family, writing, and styling hair. Growing up poor she had plenty of time to daydream about being rich one day. Nakisha comes from a large family, she grew up in the hood, that is where she

"SHYNE"

gets most of her inspiration from while she is writing her books. She started writing journals when she was in high school. Her imagination has always and forever will run wild. It was not until the year of 2015 while serving a 20year prison sentence Nakisha decided to pick up a pen and pad to start back writing again. In 2018 on her release date, she decided she would publish the books she had written. She knew for her that the sky is the limit.

You can keep up with Nakisha's new releases on Instagram at shyne_theauthor, add her on Facebook at Nakisha The Author, register an account on her website thehairmadam.com, subscribe to her YouTube channel The Hair Madam and follow her on Twitter at Nakisha The Author. Write to her at PO box1815 verona MS 38879

K

  A

    R

      M

        A

CPSIA information can be obtained
at www.ICGtesting.com
Printed in the USA
LVHW081943261021
701603LV00011B/1266